Citizens of the Night

Guy Arthur Simpson

Published by Guy Arthur Simpson, 2021.

CITIZENS OF THE NIGHT

First edition. December 20, 2021.

Copyright © 2021 Guy Arthur Simpson.

ISBN: 978-1916106109

Written by Guy Arthur Simpson.

Also by Guy Arthur Simpson

Watch for more at www.guysimpson.com.

Citizens of the Night

A t six o'clock, just as she did every morning, even though it was still night, Anja shut the front door and braced herself against the unforgiving subzero, the kind of cold to put a person in shock, before descending the steps to the street. The new security light illumined her way down then clicked off parsimoniously as soon as she reached street level. It was windless and the freshly fallen night snow glittered.

As she adjusted the neck muffler inside her zipped tracksuit with oversized mittens, Anja observed the basement studio. Shutters down and lights out, as usual. Her five-thirty message had clearly failed to raise him. Some people never make anything of themselves. They accept failure. They wallow and decline. The thought made her shiver in the gripping freeze and she stamped her feet. Well, she'd warned him. First a month and now six weeks late. No rent by five pm and he was out. She lingered a while looking at the apartment's silent door, as if it could swing open to a fanfare if it only wanted to, but had somehow forgotten how.

Anja blinked. A mist was freezing onto her face, making her small nose want to shrink further in. With a clipped, decisive *hup*, she turned and jogged off through the street's empty shadows, past dirty ice heaped in the gutters, huffing breaths that steamed when she passed under lamplight. Every thud and crunch that she made in the snow, every metronomic bob of her blonde hair, every yes, yes, yes, yes of her advance, confirmed her belief. She was going to make it. It was what she did. Hers was a bulldozing figure, small and svelte, pounding onward. Sensing her from the road, an automated delivery buggy shifted cautiously away before rolling by on its fat tyres.

· · · ·

In the basement bedsit, the lights would not come on for another two hours. Within the building, all remained blessedly quiet and her tenant snuffled contently in his sleep. He dreamed that he was standing alone at night in the shallows of an ocean, while all around him, like softly falling snow, points of white light dropped out of the sky and down to the sea, making gentle sounds as they met the surface. He cupped his hands together to catch them. Every softly shining dot that landed in his hands melted to a colour and sounded a musical note. More began to fall and faster, playing a rhapsody like some rapturous xylophone. It might have gone on everlastingly, but when he looked down the black water stared back at him with a million eyes and he felt fear. Even though he could not see them or the sandy ocean floor that they were scurrying across, he knew that two silver lobsters were coming straight for his toes. Yannick woke with a start. Tall even for a Nordic man, his feet stuck out the end of his lumpy duvet and he instinctively drew them in.

He reached for his flashing mobile.

"Today's the day," read the message.

His head fell back against the pillow. The bedsit was a lost cause. His for another few hours only. Maybe he should he just stay in. Make the most of it, do some laundry, then go and enquire at the shelters. He lay under the covers a while longer, debating between spending one last day in a warm apartment with a bed and a hot shower and giving work another go, however futile it had become.

Recently, his daily earnings as a rider had dwindled to little more than the price of a hot meal plus bike repairs. Saving towards the rent, let alone anything like a future, was a hope abandoned. If only he could wave a wand and get something better paid, but jobs just weren't there anymore. They had disappeared. Hunting down a decent one was like chasing a mythical beast through a labyrinth. Everyone said that such a thing existed—one went by just a minute ago, down that way, hurry and you might catch it—but you never quite chanced upon it. It remained just out of sight and out of reach. There were still people out there making good money. Yannick knew that because he saw them every day. He delivered their meals. If you knew the trick, there was a way in. He, though, seemed to be on the wrong side of an invisible obstruction that denied him at every turn.

On the other hand, if he didn't get on his bike, he'd be out of the only job he had. Yannick levered himself out of bed. He washed in the bathroom and combed back his long, straggly hair with his fingers. The lanky young man looking back at him in the mirror, who seemed to be developing a stoop, considered his options. It didn't take long. He hadn't any. It wasn't his landlady's fault; she'd been more than patient already. Holding his hands under the running tap in the washbasin and letting the water overflow their sides, Yannick thought of his dream. He waited for musical winking colours to drop into the swirl, waited a few seconds more and then let it go. The water gurgled and disappeared forever down the black hole.

Back in his all-purpose room, Yannick sipped some coffee, somewhat earthy after being reheated on the stove, but still good, and bit the crusty edges off a cold pizza. Still chewing, he pulled on his boots and the delivery company's bike jacket, which was so multicoloured and jazzy that, in spite of himself, it always felt like donning a superpower. The unglamorous truth was that he was being outperformed by those tea trays on wheels that ruled the streets now, the untiring automated delivery service vehicles. He took his mud-sputtered bicycle from where it leaned against the kitchenette counter and wheeled it outside.

It was still dark. It was nearly always dark now that the northern winter had closed in. Invisible snowflakes fell on his upturned face and melted in his eyes. He switched on the delivery app and waited for the earpiece to give him his first assignment.

"You are currently twenty-seventh out of twenty-seven riders," he heard out its customary way of wishing him a good morning. "To qualify for work tomorrow, don't be one of the last two! Make that extra little effort. Make the cut-off."

The map screen mounted on his handlebars lit up a route through the streets. He now had thirty minutes to pick up and deliver a birthday cake from a well-known patisserie to an address in the suburbs. Yannick gripped the bicycle handles with thermally gloved hands and shoved off into the murky metropolis.

· · · ·

The client she was with didn't know it, but Anja was concluding her second appointment of the day, helping herself to the coffee and mini-cookies provided by the owner of a kitchen and bathroom tile company as he smiled at her blue eyes more than was necessary and obligingly signed an order for the health and safety program that the law and his insurance company insisted on. An annual review of the office environment, staff briefings on safety in the workplace, a voluntary health check-up and installation of sprinklers or, as a minimum, fire extinguishers. There was a speck of fluff on his jacket lapel that she couldn't take her eyes off and longed to pick off with a fingernail. She had been glad of the assorted cookies, feeling quite ravenous, and eaten them all. As soon as his signature was on the contract and he began to talk about a fish restaurant, Anja gathered the papers into her briefcase and stood up abruptly to end the meeting. She shook his hand with an assurance that the policy was accredited and wished him a good day, leaving him looking disappointedly down at her unfinished café noir. The health and safety officer was halfway out the door when she turned on her heel and her silken scent wafted back with a sunny smile. The man's cloud lifted. She picked up the empty biscuit plate and used the paper serviette it had been sitting on to wipe the crumbs off into a wastepaper bin. Without engaging again with the ceramics man, Anja left, a flush of embarrassed satisfaction in her cheeks.

She hailed a taxi and gave it the address of her next meeting. She was coasting it. Just three more policies would fulfil her quota and she was on course for ten in these last few days before Christmas. Closing the additional contracts—those ten were certs, she estimated—would add max out her salary with bonuses, making it more than enough to cover the mortgage on the basement storage space that she had bought as an investment. If Yannick proved a surprise and came through with the rent, she could make up the deferred repayment for its conversion to an apartment. She might even renew her subscription at the gym. Presents for the family could go on her credit card. There was also the matter of a pale yellow sweater that she had been eyeing in a display window in town and that would fit her slender twenty-five-year-old form very nicely.

She checked her device, but there was nothing from her tenant. He never did contact her for that matter. She hesitated about whether to confirm dinner with Julian or to wait for him to contact her. It was only their third date and she didn't know quite how to comport herself with him. They hadn't communicated about the evening's plans since the last time, but he seemed the sort to keep to arrangements and engagements and to expect the same frame of mind from her. Seriousness. Clarity. Self-reliance. Qualities she respected. By his own account, he was an architect in great demand. He also came well-groomed and dressed very correctly. Apart from the anal sex, which he had taken as consented without actually asking her, on what was only their second date, she couldn't really fault him.

In a cheerful, polite but cheeky fashion, the self-driving taxi offered to stop off at a cafeteria that was today's sponsor. Anja chided it and told it to go straight on to her appointment.

• • • •

A little girl with a serious look on her face and a glittery hair clasp in the shape of a star opened the door and held her arms out wide for the cake box. Yannick was just about to ask how old she was today, when the girl's mother pinged an electronic confirmation of satisfactory reception at him and a "Thank you" and shut the door. A tip these days was a real achievement. A gratuity was just that: not to be expected.

His next assignment sprang up on the app. Someone wanted sushi for brunch. Well, sushi they would have and in less than half an hour. Any later than that and the delivery would be free of charge. Yannick wasn't worried about the time limit. He hadn't missed it once. The thirty-minute stipulation had been calculated with the automated delivery vehicles in mind and the ADVs, like the self-driving taxis, kept to every speed limit and always gave way to pedestrians. The ADVs might be cheaper for the delivery companies to run, and they had proliferated to the point of clogging the streets, but on a bike he was always quicker, through slush, wind or rain. Slightly hunched over and deliberate on his feet and with a tendency to plod, put him on a bicycle and Yannick fairly flew. He could swing from side to side on a snowy track and never fall. He just had to concentrate during the crucial midday dinner rush, when he stood to earn modestly well or lose big, because when the item was hot food, he got paid an extra, but deliver it late or get a complaint and the meal itself would also be free of charge and the cost docked from his earnings account.

He cut across a line of steadily moving driverless vehicles and pushed ahead of them, drawing up at a red light alongside a new type of module. It was a much sturdier ADV, of a kind he hadn't seen before, wider bodied with a stubby central flue from which steamed the flavour of mutton broth. Yannick's nostrils defied the bitter cold and breathed it in hungrily. For a few seconds, he wondered how difficult it would be to get at the food without the customer access code. Then a tempting gap opened in the cross traffic and he jumped the red light, leaving the flavoursome air and the infinitely patient and indifferent competition waiting.

• • • •

Every Tuesday, Anja had lunch with her mother, whose apartment was a couple of kilometres east of her own. They sat in the kitchen, where her mother seemed to live these days, the rest of the old-fashioned apartment with its heavy mahogany furnishing left cold and dark and empty.

"I didn't know they could find any more cuts to make," her mother said as they listened to the midday news. Provision of subsidized meals to the disabled was to be discontinued with immediate effect. When pressed on the details, the municipal council regretted that the measure would include the housebound and the blind, said the local radio. "It's wicked what they're doing. Last time it was the pensioners' heating allowance. And at Christmas of all times! What are all our taxes going on, I'd like to know? Wicked."

"That's the trouble, Mamma. There's not enough people working and paying the tax."

"Oh really!"

Her mother's exasperation matched her own, Anja thought. She chewed the home-baked bran-and-rye bread and sipped some pea soup. It was cooked with a ham bone for flavour, thick and hearty, too hot to rush. She had another five minutes.

"What's the matter with them all? Your father would have told the judge to prosecute the lot of them. Don't you be one of those quitters, Anja. Not in our family. Freeloaders is what they are."

Her father, a clerk to the district court, wanted to see everybody prosecuted, thought Anja. If he hadn't been so irascibly righteous, his heart might not have given out so soon.

The local radio continued to matter-of-factly announce a new series of cost-saving measures that would, it appeared, allow the authorities to not have to make more stringent ones. The traditional carol singing in the main square at the festooned Christmas tree below the cathedral, with hot mulled wine for adults, would go ahead as planned.

As planned? thought Anja. As *always*. To not have the singing under the tree would be like the sun going out. The town always had that, every December twenty-third, without fail. Her choir had been practising since October. They were going to contribute a carol by Dobrinka Tabakova and two traditional songs that everyone knew and could join in with. What could a few pots of punch cost?

"When Granma Osa goes back to the farmhouse after Christmas, I'm going with her."

"For how long?" asked Anja.

"I don't know. A few months, maybe."

"Months? With Granma? But you don't get on. You said so yourself. She's messy and headstrong. She doesn't have a TV and you don't read books. And what about those lumpy beds? Is she sick?"

"No, but she could do with the company. And we can share the bills. She's got geothermal there, it's cheaper."

"Oh Mamma, I can pay your heating. I'll have the downstairs rented out again soon."

"I won't dream of it. You see, that's what they do, these politicians. Now that they've messed everything up for us, their only idea is to make us foot the bill for it. They wreck families. The young are made to feel that they're responsible for everything and the old see themselves as a burden. Or vice versa. Nobody likes it, but they do it anyway and the lights go out in everybody's eyes. In any case, it's all arranged. I already have the bus tickets. I can't believe it's only three days to Christmas. Will you be bringing a boyfriend? Do stop that: those glasses are all clean. You didn't finish your soup."

"I'm just giving them a polish. You didn't use hot enough water. It leaves smears. We haven't talked about it, but I'm seeing him later. I'll let you know, okay? Give Osa a big hug from me when she gets here. I have to go. Love you, Mamma."

The afternoon slots were all follow-up inspections, They didn't count towards her quota, but she was only two new contracts short of her full target and all set to wrap up the healthy surplus before the Christmas break. She would go and buy that sweater. It would still leave her time to depilate, shower and change before meeting Julian. She would wipe the shower clean and dry with a towel, let her hair hang and sway back and forth in the blow dryer, soften her skin, straighten her back and blink in the mirror. Then be at the restaurant impeccably on time, as she always was. In the end, she had messaged him to check. She couldn't abide the untidiness of doubt.

• • • •

During the peak lunchtime hours, empty spaces between vehicles were typically difficult to find and slip through on a bicycle, but today it was worse than ever, the jammed traffic forming an unrelieved continuum. It had thickened early, with considerably more of the newer, heftier ADVs, so that Yannick had to use all his tricks to avoid being squeezed out and delayed. All four-wheeled vehicles were driverless now, irritatingly slow and predictable, and there were just so many of them. Twice on this run he had skipped onto the pavement to get past a tailback and once risked a shortcut up a one-way street against the traffic, which had paused en masse as if in displeasure, while their sensors registered an illegal manoeuvre in progress.

At the T-junction ahead, he recognized the blue-and-silver helmet of a rival delivery outfit. The rider had stopped while a nose-to-tail procession of self-drives went by. The brakes on Yannick's bicycle screeched as he pulled up next to her. They stared ahead of them. It was like watching the wagons on a train go by at a level crossing. The snow had stopped falling and a hazy fog had taken its place. The other rider was almost entirely hidden within a muffler and a scarf pulled tight over her nose. She tugged it down now to breathe more freely. They were positioned at the head of an ordered single file of vehicles. Yannick rested a foot on the kerb and looked back at them all, strung back like a line of obedient neurotics, stiff and unapproachable and secretly busy, constantly updating their maps and taking advantage of the wait to recharge batteries from power supply lines beneath the road surface.

"So what are these new tin cans all about? The big fat ones?" said Yannick.

"HotBots. That's what they're calling them. The future, mate. They're basically ovens. They prepare your meal en route. Faster and fresh from the oven. We're done, mate. Our goose is cooked."

Then the other rider was off through a gap between two minivans, with Yannick following her lead, pumping the pedals. His trousers clung cold and wet to his legs, spattered by the grubby slush that overlapped the curbs. When he reached the delivery destination, the words *our goose is cooked* were still rocking around inside his head.

The client didn't automatically sign off on the order and Yannick had to wait, panting in the thin light of the day. It had begun to darken already.

"Wait. Let me see if I like it first. Oh no, the soufflé is cold."

"It's nine degrees below zero. I got here in... seven minutes," Yannick checked the app.

"That's not my problem," she said. She handed back the starter, but held onto the main container of duck stuffed with apples and prunes.

"It can't be that cold."

"Are you calling me a liar? Oh dear."

For a moment they just stared at each other. The look on her face said that he was paying for her lunch. He knew it and she knew it. With a pained smile, she pinged his device with a dissatisfied response and withdrew to the warmth of her house.

For the remainder of his work schedule, Yannick was as if on automatic. Increasingly obstructed by the vans and passenger vehicles that trundled along inexorably on their algorithmically programmed routes, some of them cooking or keeping ready meals piping hot as they went, he knew himself to be obsolete. He might be fast but his stamina and perseverance weren't infinite and the ADV network was too well streamlined and synchronized. The riders, outnumbered, couldn't compete. Neither could they organize. There was no boss or office to plead or argue with, just an app, which pitted them against each other. When the sun set at three fifteen, with less than two hours remaining before he had to vacate the bedsit, and ranked a safe eleventh out of forty riders, Yannick decided to call it a day. It was time to go take a long, hot shower, pack his things and move on. Move out, in any case.

When he stopped at a major intersection and called up his rider account, he saw that the sum, paltry as it was after the soufflé and duck deduction, would not be credited to his bank until he had handed in his company jacket and helmet. His relationship with the company had been terminated. Somebody had complained. Attitude. The girl he had treated to lunch, presumably. Two complaints and you were out: and he already had one from inadvertently thwacking a pedestrian with his delivery pouch, causing him to bite off a disquieting length of the mustard sausage he had been nibbling.

He couldn't appeal it. The app wouldn't speak to him anymore. There was just a text message on the screen:

You have been disconnected

It really was as simple as that. There had been no contract, no social security credits, no holiday allowance, just a trifling payment per delivery in an unsatisfactory arrangement that he was now barred from. If only they had the decency to sack him, thought Yannick. To be disconnected reminded him horribly of his mother in hospital, when her useless life support systems were closed down and unplugged.

Jacking high the heel of his left boot, he put all his frustration into it and kicked over one of the smaller, older ADVs that idled alongside him at the red light. And immediately felt bad about it. An antenna promptly swivelled round and photographed him. Oh no, he thought. Facial recognition. He knew all about this.

"You have been identified, Y.B.," it addressed him by his initials.

Yes, it had him.

"Do you want to pay a spot fine of eighty crowns now for criminal damage with malicious intent, or go before a magistrate later and risk more? You just spoiled a lasagne and bent my wing."

"Go ahead and take it," he said.

"Is that answer: 'I want to pay a spot fine of eighty crowns now'? Reply 'yes' or 'no'."

"Yes. You know it is."

"The QR code's on my rear screen."

Yannick dismounted and went to the back of the toppled ADV where he crouched down, holding his bike up with one hand and directing his mobile with the other to scan the QR code that was displaying. The money vanished from his bank account, leaving it wiped out.

"It was nothing personal," he told the vehicle.

To prove it, he laid his bike on the ground and pulled the buggy back onto its wheels. There was a crumpled dent and a crack in the chrome trim, but it would be okay. He switched off the delivery service app for the last time and looked up and down long, indistinct roads that led nowhere. The wild goose chase was over. He had tried and he had failed. All he had to show for slogging his way through another three weeks of dead-end work were two low-denomination banknotes, which some outlets still accepted, and a state of unmitigated resignation. He was cold, wet and destitute. What was he to do? If nobody else cared, why should he?

Cycling the city with focussed intensity for several hours a day had made him quite familiar with its residential and commercial districts. He knew, for example, that he was five streets due east of the grand old square that dominated the capital's southern reaches, and that between here and there was an arcade of businesses, including a licensed liquor store which opened all day. He found the storefront, wheeled round, secured his bicycle to a lamppost and went inside.

The shop, which had an employee working behind an old-fashioned counter, was brightly lit and almost oppressively warm. Festive hampers and expensive bottles of whisky were decorated with tinsel. One wall held pink and blue gin and vodka bottles on glass shelves, backlit above stacked shiny boxes of liqueur chocolates. Yannick bought a bottle of aquavit and stashed it in his delivery pouch. He rated the service with five stars, thanked the unresponsive employee and replaced his gloves before going out to be struck again by the familiar if hideous cold.

At the main square, which was nearby, he pushed his bike as far as a wrought-iron bench. He cleared the snow off with one arm of his thick coat and sat down to drink his prize. At this time of year, the monumental plaza, laid with stone flags and set round with sober, floodlit edifices, the Town Hall, the high cathedral wall and a row of exclusive boutiques, was constantly busy with shoppers drifting between department stores and gift shops, holding onto the memory and promise of hope and prosperity. The precinct was supposed to be traffic-free, but electric scooters slalomed between townspeople laden with boxes and bags. In one corner, between official buildings and the cathedral steps, an ice rink had been set up. Yannick watched the backs of bulkily insulated parents watching their children in an annual ritual matched only by the queuing faithful in the courtyard above, who stood and waited dutifully to enter the medieval church. The schnapps tasted sharp. He drank it down and then some more, leaning his head back. Rising high above all the hustle and bustle, the traditional, illuminated Christmas tree, tall and mighty, sparkled its colours. Two evenings from now, a throng of his fellow citizens would assemble under the tree to sing carols and share hot drinks and snacks of figs and roast chestnuts, raising voices and smiles to the very tip of the straight-backed fir where a lone star sparkled, pointing beyond the cathedral roof to the sunless firmament.

Yannick felt almost cheerful. With nothing in the world but small change and his black-and-white bicycle, he was strangely unconcerned, if hungry. There was a van nearby selling spit-roasted chickens that he couldn't afford, but he couldn't face the unwanted cold soufflé, either. In the end, he settled for another swig on the bottle and the contemplation that it infused in him.

Opposite him stood a kiosk that sold lottery tickets for the blind. They weren't going to get fed, either. No more meal deliveries for them: he had read about their plight on the newsfeed. It must be like being confined to a sentry box all day, he thought, looking at the narrow booth. It was hexagonal, painted forest green and topped by an iron ball of the same colour. Winning numbers were posted in a little window over which a red digital read-out advertised the Christmas lottery and its pay-out in the millions. Yannick wandered over and pushed the two small banknotes he had left under the window. Was it enough? The shadowy figure behind smoked glass shook its head. Not for the Yule lotto, the big moneyspinner, no. He could have a scratch card. They paid out in cash. Did he want one? Yes, said Yannick, who took the card and his change from the marble counter and went back to the bench. He unscrewed the bottle cap of his aquavit and took another mouthful. It suffused him nasally with caraway and fennel and burned nicely on the way down.

There had been a blind man on one of the training courses he had been obliged to take during his last period of unemployment. No courses meant no credits. No credits meant no food vouchers. If the worst came to the worst, it meant no right to shelters. Like many other jobless, Yannick had done them all, no matter how absurd. The disabled were no longer exempt from these self-improvement drives and the blind man was supposed to train as an electrician. On a study course of thirteen modules, from how to wire a plug through to safety measures relating to high tension pylons. To match coloured cables together and not get electrocuted. Fortunately, the only hands-on activity with live current was in Module Five, by which time the teacher knew not to expect much of the quiet, intense individual behind dark glasses in the second row and didn't ask him to stick his fingers in the circuit. Otherwise, the course was heavily theory-based and in any case, as long as the man was there he got his attendance confirmed. Simply turning up and being in the room was enough to get the course accredited and the employment service boxes ticked. Not that the knowledge and skills learned on the course were going to get any of them into work. The teacher told them with a mixture of pride and apology that hand-held devices were now able to diagnose and repair so much better than trained humans. You held it up to the junction box and it could image the entire electrical network of an apartment or office, identify the problem and solve ninety-nine per cent of the faults.

"I can do that."

Everyone had looked at the blind man. It was the first time he had spoken up.

"I can picture networks in my head. Distances. Connections. I can tell you the way from the Queen Beatrix Baby Clinic to the municipal cemetery with my eyes closed."

He then laughed out loud and long at his own joke and the teacher was so kerfuffled that she lost track of where she was and had to consult her notes.

"Module Nine," the blind man prompted her. "Signals and systems. Fourier series. Let's get onto the heavy duty stuff. Power generation. Let's go nuclear!"

If the man spoke with a somewhat disrespectful levity, he had a point, Yannick thought. For the enthusiastic course leader, it was about imparting what she knew, but for them it was a charade. Nobody in the room was going to be advanced by this training: the teacher had just admitted as much. The same went for any of the compulsory courses that promised access to gainful employment. Software directing dextrous machines could do the job so much better. Data analysis, digital marketing, financial administration, sales promotion, carpentry, food allergy management, evaluation of environmental impact, personal shopping, real estate, manicures, fork lift truck driver, cook, mechanic, agricultural manager, business intelligence, hairdressing: they could all be performed more efficiently and cheaply by artificial intelligence allied to new developments in technology. The robotic capability for fixing leaking pipes in a wall wasn't quite there yet, but plumbers and other manually skilled professionals were increasingly being recruited to program diagnostics into machines that would eventually replace them.

If Yannick's habitual condition was one of dejection, he, too, had a point. When his mother died of lymphatic cancer, his father had waited all of four months before selling the family home, a well-maintained three-bed condominium, and moving "semi-permanently" to Costa Rica. To his bewildered son, he awarded enough to cover the short-term rental of a smaller unit, wherever he chose to relocate, plus any item he wanted from the apartment. "It's time you stood on your own two feet," he announced. "You can come and visit when you're ready." Yannick took his bicycle and books, a collection of outdated DVDs and his mother's Japanese maple bonsai. He didn't know what his father meant by being "ready", but he did understand that he was about to find himself alone in the world and wondering how he was going to survive.

He was right to wonder. Something of a loner, Yannick now in his mid-twenties discovered loneliness. His childhood home sold and his family gone, Yannick moved to a spick-and-span if cramped studio apartment closer to the city centre. After putting down the key deposit he found that he had enough left over to pay the rent including heating oil for six months, but nothing else, not even food.

Uncomplaining, finding his father's exit perplexing rather than upsetting, and not wanting to ask anyone he knew for help, he had cycled around the new neighbourhood to see if there were any for hire notices at shops or yards (there weren't any), and knocked on doors in to ask if anyone wanted snow shovelling (nobody did). Yannick applied himself more seriously. Listing himself as a graduate open to all offers on employment websites, he found himself wanted. Indeed, he was accepted for one job after another, but the promising incursions into the world of work took the nature of brief engagements that ended in his expulsion. Three times he found and started jobs, only to be discontinued four weeks later. Sandwich bar, department store and garden centre each took him on with alacrity, and each on a trial period that ended with depressing predictability on the day that the law would have obliged him to be paid. It was like pushing with all his might into a wall of elastic which gave obligingly, letting him further and further in, only to catapult him back out again when he reached the limit.

Yannick was no good with his hands, little better with people, and a whole series of jobs, from the development, marketing and manufacture of a product to its transportation, its stocking on shop shelves and the check-out where you paid for it, were all automated nowadays.

The one occupation he was qualified to do no longer existed. Librarianship was just one more profession overtaken by the considerably more cost-effective and smarter service provided by intelligent machines. No sooner had he obtained his diploma than libraries up and down the country switched over en bloc to a single, national computerized system and job offers for newly graduated librarians were reduced to nil.

Then he had a break.

An alert on his mobile advised him of an opportunity to work six days a week on reception and security at a high-flying tech company. University level and a clean record but no experience required. He applied and within seconds a green tick told him that the position was his.

It was a company that guarded its new developments closely. To enter the busy building, every employee had to swipe a card to pass through a turnstile in the ground floor lobby. A random sample would have their face matched by Yannick to their photo. Any visitors had to be authorized by a senior manager and met by a member of staff, who would act as escort. Only then would Yannick let the visitor through by pressing a button to open the gate next to his assault-proof control box. Deliveries had to be collected from the entrance foyer by the employee responsible.

After just a few days, Yannick was on friendly greeting terms with a number of the staff, starting to recognize them and know their names. He kept an eye on the screens that showed the street outside, the foyer, the lift area on each floor and the emergency exits. When the evening shift came in and before he went off duty, he did the rounds of each floor, checking the offices, meeting spaces and washrooms. For a while, he thought that he had charmed his way into the privileged world of work. No technical problems had arisen, staff entered and exited smoothly, goods were admitted securely and no incidents had occurred.

After one month, the CEO of the company emerged from the elevator followed by the other four board directors. Already somewhat conditioned by his role of officer on duty, Yannick found himself standing at some sort of pointless attention behind his reinforced glass windows. It was unusual to see the bosses here; they had their own private entrance at the rear. Instead of leaving the building, the company directors stayed back, watching as a group. What were they looking at? There was nothing happening. Yannick switched his audio feed to the hidden microphone monitoring the inner foyer area, and listened in.

"This is just it, you see," he heard the Chief Executive say. He motioned over a newly arrived male technician, who had just entered through the electronic barrier, and who now took off his cap, peeled off a rubber mask and unzipped his coat to reveal a confident-looking young woman that Yannick had never seen before.

What could be going on?

Yannick turned up the volume on his speaker.

"Our mission statement defines our company as tech enterprise at the cutting edge and here we are being failed by human error at our very gates."

The CEO then played his fellow directors a video on his mobile. It showed one occasion when their security guard had waived protocol and allowed in a senior manager who had forgotten his pass, and another when he waved through two girls who had arrived late and tipsy from a lunchtime birthday drink.

"He's so shaggy," said one of the directors. "Lugubrious. What's he doing here?"

"It's faulty, it's antiquated, and one day it could be costly," he told them. "We have the software ready to go. It's time to roll it out. Biometrics with facial recognition is a security no-brainer. You install it once and it immediately starts paying for itself. The Town Hall has adopted it already: we trialled it for them two weeks ago and it's still in operation. Two government ministries have put in an order, so has the airport authority. The stores are going to love it. They can ID customers and target them with personalized shopping recommendations."

Shortly after the bosses had returned by the elevator to their top floor suites, Yannick received a request from the building supervisor to report to her office.

"I'm sorry. You've been AI'd," the woman told him.

He hadn't heard the expression before, but it didn't take much explaining. The problem, Yannick realized, was that he was human. Faulty and antiquated. They just couldn't afford to keep him on.

"So I'm fired?"

"Technically, no. You haven't completed the probationary period, so the company is simply releasing you."

• • • •

"I lost my job," he said later that day, when his landlady opened her apartment door after buzzing him up. "I thought I ought to tell you in person that I can't pay the rent."

He was already a month late and the tech company had docked his first and only pay in lieu of the professional training that he had apparently just received.

For a few seconds, the young woman was silent. It was the first time that they had spoken since a neighbourly occasion when they had watched a movie together, and accumulated thoughts and calculations seemed to be rushing through her head.

"I can give you a month to find it," she said at last.

Until December twenty-first, then. The winter solstice.

"Thanks," he said, and the interview was over. He turned and went back downstairs to his bedsit. The simple friendliness with someone of his own age that they had shared that one time was no longer appropriate. Somehow it seemed unfair that she should be so fair. In both senses of the word. He put some coffee on to brew and sighed to himself.

At the Social Security Office, a greying, bespectacled lady informed him that he needed to work for another thirteen months in order to receive minimum subsidy. If he did full-time courses, he could apply for food vouchers, but he wouldn't be in receipt of monetary payments, of course. Yannick shook his head. No, he needed to have income.

"Use your resources. What can you do? Are you alright?" she enquired kindly. "You know a doctor's note attesting incapacity for reasons of mental ill-health can still justify a temporary benefit."

"Do I look that bad?" he said. "Could I bring that to you personally?"

"I won't be here," she said. "Nor will anybody else. The service is going digital after the holiday break."

"That's too bad. I hope you can process your own claim."

The woman smiled weakly. "My cats will be happy," she said.

Yannick's doctor waved him away. "No weight loss, no suicidal thoughts, no self-harming, no sleepless nights: there's nothing there," he pointed out. "You're grieving, but that's normal. Maybe you're depressed. It's hard to say. Chin up, young man. You have your whole life ahead of you."

Shown the door by the city, Yannick looked outside of it for inspiration. To the west and north, spreading out in a broad, green arc, was pristine forest and running through it were well-kept cycling tracks. One item Yannick did have, which he cared for better than himself, was a decent bicycle. He decided that fresh air and fitness would get him out of his rut. Breathe life and hopefulness into him.

It didn't. He pushed himself for hour after hour through the pines and firs, but it didn't make him feel any better. He always ended up back where he started, a place where nothing made sense. His bicycle tyres bit into the mud track and the rut deepened. His only two real friends were no longer in town. One had married and moved away. The other was a technician on a film crew, who posted images on social media of Australia and Fiji, of barbecues and coral reefs, but also sharks and saltwater crocodiles. It made Yannick think of his father, who might as well have been swallowed up by some such predator in Central America. He hadn't heard from him once.

One evening, utterly bored and glum, feeling boxed in by the basement bedsit and wondering if he should get in touch with an old girlfriend who had chain-smoked and shouted at him a lot, he bit into a large snack of toasted cheese and thought: yes! Not to the girl, who nonetheless appealed for the unbridled sex they had had together, but to the food. The food industry, to be precise. The fish-smoking factories by the coast were all robotic now. So were the mechanical burger flippers at fast food outlets, the pizza loaders, bakers, cutters and packagers. But the hot food still needed delivering and it was here that Yannick saw an opening. Use your resources, the lady with the cats had said. The bicycle was it and he was good on it.

The first courier service that he contacted took him on as a rider immediately and gave him razzle-dazzle livery in which to perform. An opportunity had opened. For three non-stop, physically demanding and poorly paid weeks, while he had conveyed food, food and more food, the opening had widened steadily, until today when it had slammed shut.

Two policemen were walking across the square. Yannick belched and hastily stuffed the bottle into a deep pocket of his coat. When they walked past, he tried not to smile too much. They looked at him, but didn't stop. I probably look suitably seasonally decorative, he supposed, in my coat of many colours and rosy cheeks.

Yannick relaxed. Which is to say: he gave up. His legs had already stopped running after an illusory reward and now his mind gave up the chase, also. "I am not unhappy," he explained out loud to the shoppers. "I am unplugged." His mind had become as clear as the aquavit. He wasn't, he saw, emotionally disturbed, and his alienation from regular human existence and society wasn't a feeling: it was a fact. The economic model simply held no place for him.

He wasn't alone. Under the grey stone wall that rose up to the cathedral courtyard huddled a strung-out line of homeless. They were sheltering as best they could beneath a continuous patchwork of covers, clothing, umbrellas and cardboard that made them look like a single, multi-jointed creature. They could be an out-of-work pantomime caterpillar, thought Yannick, touting for a role in a festive play. He was one step from joining them. Or was that step behind him already? Where was there for him to go but down? From bum on a bench to a bum on the ground. He shivered. The arctic freeze of the night was descending and the stark lights of the public concourse made his situation cruelly explicit. He could sell his bike. He would *have* to sell his bike. That would leave him with a little cash, two sets of clothes, some books and DVDs, and a bonsai tree.

It's my mess and no one can take it away from me, Yannick asserted, banging the bottle on the bench. He couldn't find it in him to blame his father for seeking a bright, new life in the tropics, with the parrots and the waving palms and the sun. The benefit of experience, together with the proceeds of the condominium, he nodded to himself approvingly.

What I really need, he thought, is a piss. He leaned forward to lever himself up and something fell to the ground. He picked it up. It was the lottery ticket. He pulled off a glove and used a fingernail to scratch off the concealed result on the card. There was a figure in the small rectangular box, but he had made good inroads into the bottle of schnapps and couldn't read it. He looked more closely, with just one eye, holding it up to the light. He had won. He had bloody won. Quite a lot. Not a fortune, but yeah, enough to pay off his rent debt. Bloody hell, she might let him stay on for another month. Yannick stood up and rocked on his feet. Blurred, everything was blurred. He still held the bottle of aquavit in his left hand. He wanted a piss and some of that chicken. The ticket. He aimed for the kiosk, which was now a beacon of hope in a swelling, quaking square. A hand must have been shaking the sky because snow was falling out of it. "Sorry," said Yannick, when a perfumed lady told him to watch where he was going. When the lights went out in the square, it didn't deter him. He was only a few steps from the kiosk and the momentum carried him there like a sleepwalker.

"I won," he said to the darkness.

"I can't pay out. The system's down," said the man.

"But it's just cash. Can't you just check the number?

"No. Come back another time."

"I've got a flashlight on..." my mobile, thought Yannick, then realized that he was talking to a blind man, who needed to scan the barcode on the ticket.

Yannick couldn't see a thing, either. All the lights were out. Every single one. The square was strangely quiet, hesitant and imposing. People wandered or stood still with faces eerily lit by their mobiles, talking into them, asking questions as if requesting instructions in a game.

In the dark it seemed even colder. He could feel more snow on his face and a rising wind. Yannick felt a sudden need to be reunited with his bicycle which leaned against the bench just a few steps behind him, but unsecured. He turned his back on the iron kiosk, walked forwards holding out his arms and whacked his shin against a pedal of the bicycle, which he grabbed as he fell to the ground, pulling it on top of him. It hurt. He didn't want to get up. With his hip aching, Yannick's attention went instinctively to the bottle in his pocket, which he was thankful to find unbroken. He decided that another swig was in order just in case it happened again.

When he was able to push the bike up and off, leaning it back against the bench, he got back to his feet and blinked and blinked again. A black nothing. Not even a gleam in the night sky. Just the hidden weight of the world and the giant tree looming invisibly. There were the small sounds of people talking and seeking a way out of the square, but no one nearby. He wondered if he could get away with it and then did. He unzipped his trousers and let loose the frustration. With sad gladness, as the world obliterated revolved around his inebriation, he stood at the country's epicentre and urinated warmly into the void. "I am released," he whispered.

It was everyone else's turn to find themselves in an unintelligible predicament. The benighted square was still a tangled net of Christmas shoppers, business people, residents and store workers, town hall staff and families with children. Yannick's countrymen and women prided themselves on their civic-mindedness and they were going about the set-back with customary self-possession. All the same, this was a bit extreme. A gelid shadow passed through their midst, unseen but felt by all. Whether they turned a blind eye or not, they were on the receiving end each day of what was going on. The shortages. The neglect. The lay-offs. Their jobs being feasted on by technological monsters. Yet the habit of confidence and sobriety was tenacious. Even if they knew in their hearts that it was all going downhill and this Christmas sustained only by denial and festive nostalgia, the people would not be robbed of it. The power outage was inconvenient and couldn't be ignored, much as they would wish, but a little patience and the lights would come back on. Homes and families awaited them. Their society was robust. Institutions were built to last.

Common facts remained facts. It was December twenty-first and it was a relieved, redundant librarian who righted his bicycle and got astride it.

He put the lamp on and got moving. Another fact that was a fact: lamp or no lamp, he couldn't see where he was going. The handlebar lurched around independently of his grip and he narrowly missed a pair of walking clergy, a lumpy shadow errant in the worldly square. It was a lucky miss, because if they were guided by divination, Yannick wasn't. He got off the bike before the inevitable happened. Two scooters crisscrossed before him like fireflies, briefly exposing the lottery kiosk like some obelisk in the desert and Yannick made for the only point of reference he had. He stashed the bottle beside the booth before wheeling the bicycle off in as straight a line as he could imagine until he hit one of the four walls of the square and turned left. Sinister was as good as dexter in a maze. In an undisclosed distance, he could make out hints of lights from manual two-wheelers, the only traffic that was still functioning. As he exited the square, he took out his mobile and shone its weakening flashlight on the street name. you are here, he thought. Well, if he couldn't see the way, he could remember it. Memory would stand in for manifest reality and get him there, even if the only place he had to go was the one he could no longer call home.

. . . .

She had never seen such a romantic setting. The whole restaurant was lit by candles and dark with mystery. Tables were separated by intimate boundaries of shade and each was centre-set with four red roses and a single, gently burning candle. Anja suppressed observations of poor practice and infringements of health and safety regulations and gave in to the sensuality. She walked a long stucco wall, heat exuding from the shadows, waiters projecting like statues in the chiaroscuro. The distant hum of an underground generator was all but muted by the crimson carpeting.

"Hi! This is beautiful!"

"Hi," Julian looked up then checked his watch. "I ordered us a starter. I hope that's alright."

"Of course," she smiled, undoing the big buttons on her white coat as he stabbed a rolled herring.

"Ya. And some sparkling spring water."

Anja thought her green dress might leave him if not speechless at least impressed. She had splashed out and bought it together with the yellow sweater, which lay folded in its paper bag at the bottom of her overnight bag. She leaned back in her chair and smoothed herself down.

"What do you think?" she caught his eye.

"Hm. Expensive, ya?"

"For a special occasion."

A third date was kind of special, she thought.

He nodded.

"How—"

"Ho—"

They said.

"You," Julian waved his fork.

"No, you," she insisted.

"How far along are you on your quota this month?"

A waiter, seeing her stare in his direction, hurried towards their table, but she shook her head.

"Good. In fact, I only need two—"

"Did I tell you—I have to tell you this—the Department of Industry has shortlisted my design for their new offices? The original work is paid for, of course, but it would be a major contract and quite a feather in my cap. If it goes ahead."

This time Anja did beckon the waiter, who brought menus printed on laminated card that were at least three times larger than they needed to be.

"Congratulations. I'm proud of you. You must be."

"It's early to say, but ya. Senior partner," he supposed.

Anja suddenly felt her position to be a very lowly one. She would have to push for a managerial role. As the company's top sales performer, she had a right to stake a claim.

"I got the tickets," she wiggled her phone, blushing immediately. The prospective boss was adopting the behaviour of a secretary. He wouldn't respect that.

"It starts at seven-thirty, correct?"

"Ya. Yes."

"Some nudity, I think!"

"I believe so. The theatre must turn up the heating for the duration."

Julian indicated to the waiter that they were ready to order.

He might not have heard her, but in any case Anja decided not to make any more attempts at humour.

"Speaking of which my apartment is a short ride afterwards, if you are free," he said.

"Well…" she found herself blushing again. She was keen to engage in sex, but it would be only their second time and the first had involved anal penetration that she hadn't been prepared for. It had caused her to cut short her morning run.

She wanted to request that he abstained, but this wasn't the moment. She certainly wasn't going to mention that she had packed her running kit in her silver shoulder bag, together with fresh knickers, just in case.

"I'll have the salmon, with boiled potatoes."

"Ah, good old-fashioned girl. Meatballs," Julian told the waiter. "And some more water. Or would you like a glass of wine?"

"No, no. Water is good."

"That's settled, then," he said.

"Can I ask you something?"

The subject of her question straightened up, clearly interested. He had the most piercing blue eyes she had ever seen. They weaponized his masculinity, which she could not find issue with. His suit looked brand new and the bright pink tie chosen as carefully as his date.

"How long would you give a tenant who was behind on the rent?"

Julian looked annoyed. "A rental agreement stipulates that eviction proceedings may commence if rent is not paid during the first five days of the month. Three weeks ago."

"You don't think I should allow leeway?" It was a month and three weeks, in fact, but she didn't mention that.

"No. The law is for a reason. It's the same for everyone."

"Still, it is Christmas."

"Anja, it is always some date or other. These people spin a story to make you feel sorry for them and just take advantage of you. You work hard for what you have. You deserve it."

"We agree, then. Good," she sipped her water. "It's good that we can talk like this. About everything, you know."

He nodded.

"This guy, the tenant, he's odd. He barely talks at all. I think he's just shy."

"When were you talking?

"Oh, one evening he came up with an old movie: a DVD. Do you remember them? I didn't know people still had them. About a submarine stranded on the ocean floor."

"He was just trying to get into your pants. Did he?"

"No! I'm his landlady."

"You're so naive," said Julian.

"He barely said a word all evening. Then he thanked me and went back down to the bedsit."

"The studio apartment."

"Yes, I know. But it's a bedsit. A garage conversion."

"A weirdo. Lonely. You have to be watch it with those types."

"I suppose you're right."

"Ya."

Anja rapped her knuckles on the tabletop three times. The same hand wanted to pick up a knife and do the same on her empty wine glass, which would immediately summon the sommelier, and she hurriedly countermanded the frivolity. She looked at Julian and concentrated on smiling.

The sailors in the sunken submarine, which was cloaking its position with radio silence, had communicated with each other by tapping on the steel hull until the captain halted them angrily. Enemy warships could triangulate even the faintest of sounds and depth charge them.

It was quite good. Anja liked plots with clear-cut problems to be worked out.

Yannick said, imagine people doing that today, sending messages like that, coded in little rhythms. Across a café, for example. Instead of searching for each other online. He picked up a pen and made a tip-tip-tippity-tap with it on Anja's IKEA table.

"Let's watch," she had said.

With oxygen depleted to gasping level and battery power almost out, to save his men the submarine captain had raised the vessel to the surface where a warship had taken them prisoner, while the captain stayed behind to scupper his command. The submarine raised its long grey hull like some forlorn sea mammal and sank for the last time, its crew looking on, and the credits rolled.

Yannick had got to his feet and thanked Anja for her hospitality, taking with him his ejected DVD and amiable diffidence. "Cool jacket," she had said. It was that, a technicolour dreamcoat wowing her white-and-beige apartment, and he had actually smiled as he left. He was a nice enough chap. He just needed a haircut, new clothes and some motivation, she thought. That night, she had stayed awake a while in bed, listening to see if he might make little knocks from below to say thanks again. Shortly afterwards, he had been made redundant. On telling her, she'd offered him four extra weeks to pay the rent. When he didn't contact her, or call by again, she knew that he wasn't going to make it.

"Anyway, he'll be gone. I gave him until five pm this afternoon to pay. It's way past that now," she checked her mobile.

"Quite right. You're not a charity."

"He lost one job as security guard and now he's doing food deliveries on a bike."

"What a loser. Well, he'll be out of that job soon."

"What do you mean?"

"The new economy is all about automatons, schatz. You develop them or you manage them. You can't be one."

She looked outside. Even the darkness could not hide the wet snow, falling as if in haste. It didn't look welcoming out there.

• • • •

The power cut had knocked out the network which directed all the four-wheeled traffic and the only movement and the only lights came from a few cyclists and the occasional electronic scooter. The passenger vehicles, merchandise vans and other assorted ADVs were out of action and sleeping, rooted to the spot where they had been when their real time programming and underground power supply were switched off. Jettisoned passengers were traipsing the pavement, hugging the line of buildings in single file, while who knew how many more remained trapped inside their transports. Snow was starting to adhere to the rounded shadows of the larger ADVs, the HotBots, which looked massive on the avenue. It was like passing by lifeless elephantine seals on a long beach running through the city. Yannick weaved through them in the virtual obscurity, wobbling occasionally. He turned right onto a narrow street where there were no wandering people and he had to negotiate a tight obstacle course of halted traffic, kerbs, trees, signposts, lampposts, fire hydrants and recycling units. It was, Yannick found, quite fun.

He had regained a measure of focus and balance as the bicycle lamp showed him the future two metres at a time. He reached his apartment building, dismounted and went down the steps to the basement.

He couldn't get in. He pressed his electronic key and pushed the door, but the lock didn't open. Either Anja had changed the key code, which made sense seeing as he was way past the deadline for vacating, or the lock was dependent on the apartment's power supply, which was down here as it was all over the city. He went back up to the street and round to the steps that led up to the building's main door. The security light sprang on using its battery back-up and Yannick stopped in his tracks, shocked by the glare. As his eyes adjusted, he beheld a staircase with double balustrade so perfectly exhibited for his convenience—the one and only piece of the world in bright, visible splendour—that it looked like a stage prop for him to run up and claim the crown that had been waiting for him all along. He slogged up in his soggy boots and trousers and pushed Anja's buzzer. It didn't work. He pressed the buzzers for the other apartments. Nothing. He banged on the door, but if anybody was at home, they weren't going to open up to his hammering.

He took a couple of steps back and looked up at the windows. There was a glimmer behind the curtains on the second floor, but Anja's apartment on the first showed no signs of life. What was he to do? He was in no fit state to call her and explain himself intelligibly and he couldn't wait indefinitely in the hope that she might come home. He would freeze to death from hypothermia first. He took off a glove and fished out the lottery ticket from his back trouser pocket between two numb fingers. He checked his other pockets then the delivery pouch, where he found a stubby pen, wrote a quick message on the back of the scratch card and dropped in her mail box. They were quits. He was twenty krona short, but she had said she'd pay him that much for having swept the snow from their street front.

He went back to his bike to make the return trip to the square, partly because he planned to ask the homeless the address of a shelter, partly because he had left the bottle there and he was sobering up. Neither offered much promise, but it was all had left. He was very cold and he needed to get moving again.

• • • •

"This is a first, though, isn't it?" Anja said, referring to the blackout. "My taxi just stopped halfway here, opened the doors and wouldn't respond when I asked it what it was doing. As if we'd had an argument. I had to walk the rest of the way in the dark." No small feat in these shoes, she wanted to add. "Sorry I was late." She was never late.

"Only five minutes. I was lucky. I was just over the road, being groomed," said Julian.

Anja wondered which part of him had received the honour. His nails were buffed but so was the rest of him. It could have been anywhere.

"What do you think happened?" she asked.

"How should I know? No idea," he gave a little shrug.

"But if it's the nuclear power station?" said Anja. "Like Chernobyl?"

"I think we'd know about it already," Julian said, waving his mobile without looking up from his meatballs.

• • • •

The square was ominously deserted when Yannick got back. It didn't feel like a public space anymore. On the far side, armed police barricades had sprung up around the Town Hall and the other government buildings. Flashes from the search lamps on their helmets strafed the generalized emptiness, bouncing off the wet flagstones and the cathedral wall, now vacant of its derelicts. Where the homeless had been, there wasn't a trace. They and their detritus had been cleared out. But there, Yannick saw, as another flash swept round like a lighthouse to point it up, was the kiosk. And there was his bottle, next to the kiosk door. With no one to ask, his chances of finding a shelter had diminished, but he would settle for a bird in the hand.

As he picked it up by its neck, he heard muffled sounds coming from inside the kiosk. Some shuffling and dragging, then a thump. There was no point going back to the window and arguing about his ticket, which wasn't even his anymore, but he did wonder what the lottery seller was still doing in there until the penny dropped: the blind man might not have noticed the blackout. All he would know was that the scanner, with its affirmative or negative beeps, was offline. The joke is on all of us, Yannick thought. If the blind only knew it, things had just been evened up a little bit and it was more their territory than ours now. They were an odd collective, Yannick thought. They didn't see you and you didn't see them, forced into institutional dependency or these cramped boxes that stood all over the city, inert street furniture that he never really registered—until now, when it had become his lightless lodestar and he found himself clinging to it. A marginalized person might know something, he supposed. He might even know about shelters. Yannick screwed the top back on the bottle and felt his way around the hexagonal walls. When he arrived at the window, he shone his mobile inside.

There was nobody. Just a narrow stool behind the marble counter. Where was he? He hadn't left through the door. Or had he? Maybe when blind people came out of their kiosks, people with sight couldn't see them. Now that he thought about it, he had never seen a blind person go in or come out of one. He did, however, see something. An opportunity. It could be a private shelter, however short-lived, from the murderous cold of the northern night, in which a wind was now picking up. He had a good kick in his boot, he knew that. Hand over hand, he edged round to the door and stood back from it. He listened first, to make sure that he was quite alone in this local black bubble, and then put his heavy-boned frame into it, striking hard with his heel.

The door buckled. He kicked again. Three, four. The reports rang out like shots, echoing round the stone square, but he couldn't stop. Five, and on six it broke open. He could hear running across the square. Once he got inside, the space was tiny. There was nowhere to hide. He sat on the floor and pushed the ticket seller's stool against the door with his feet, as if that would stop assault police from breaking in. Shouts were already coming. Boots, quite a lot of them, running hard. He flicked on his mobile. The stool. A wastepaper basket in the corner. Nothing else. He flicked it off again. Wait: there was something else. On the floor. What had it been? Too late. They were here, outside. It was almost as if he could feel their hurried, hot breathing, their violent minds, as they went past, not stopping, spreading out over the whole plaza, not knowing where the shooter might be. Yannick held his breath and risked it again with the mobile light. One long second that turned into two by mistake until the illuminated screen snapped off. The something he had seen was interesting and not on the floor, but part of it. The steel plate that he had pushed the stool off had a pair of hinges. Yannick moved his knees apart and got his fingers under the square lid. When he lifted it up and felt underneath there was nothing. Just air. Under cover of the heavy lid, he clicked on the mobile once more.

There was a fixed metal ladder going down a vertical shaft.

Some decisions are made for you. He hadn't done much wrong, but fear told him that the police might not see it that way. He propped the steel lid against the stool and let the opening swallow him like a snake. When a foot found a rung, he took firm hold of the ladder and made his way slowly down.

• • • •

Her morning run the next day was from Julian's apartment to her own. With the smart system controlling and powering motorized transport still out, it was the only way she could get home or anywhere else in the city. He had got unenthusiastically out of bed at five thirty and fetched her his head torch, while she put on the running gear from her bag and stashed her evening wear in its place.

She was used to having the sidewalk to herself at this early hour, but not the roads as well. She padded along the night's broad thoroughfares past the spookily halted vehicles. The snow had stopped falling and it was peaceful.

Her mind went over the events of the previous evening, looking for a feeling to string together a meaningful narrative from its elements, yet unable to figure out what it might be. Dinner: a gorgeous place, unforgettable. Theatre: they should have left. His present: fantastic. Sex: they were new to each other, still learning.

Just recalling the ambience of the restaurant steeped her in a rich, warm glow. Perhaps she had talked too much. Being late had put her in a strange mood.

They were late, also, for the play, having to walk there, and the performance had been insensible to anyone with normal sight and hearing. Unlike the plush restaurant, the theatre had no generator and the candles placed on stage had failed to illuminate the gestures of naked actors who were visibly suffering in the cold. Their mini-microphones were also inoperative, so that one couldn't hear what they said, only perceive their many shrieks and infrequent laughter.

By the time they got to Julian's, where the central heating wasn't working either, she was ready to jump straight into bed, but he had insisted on making Himalayan tea, which he set before her on a tray, with a large envelope bearing her name propped against the porcelain teapot. It was an early Christmas present, he had explained, seeing as he couldn't see her until the twenty-seventh, when they could meet at six pm.

When she opened it, her heart popped. It was a year's pass for two people to the most exclusive spa hotels in the country. Four nights per month in famed forest beauty spots and by the coast. Just the extras cost a mint, but even they were included on the first visit.

Sex had been non-anal by her request and acceptable, but reminded her of when she first met him at the gym and he had been on an exercise machine. She decided to let it pass. When she asked him, "How do you feel about us?" He had replied "Good, ya ya," made himself comfortable and gone to sleep.

Anya reached her street, switched to the middle of the road to go round an ill-defined human figure and was about to run up the steps to the front door with a *hup* when the security light failed to come on. The battery had run out. She mounted the steps with care and found that she had to use the mechanical keys to get into the building and her apartment. The boiler having been off for over twelve hours, the rain shower wasn't just tepid, it was proper cold and Anja found herself exclaiming like the actors the previous evening, but not to shower was out of the question. She rubbed herself down with a fresh towel, worried about her hair which she couldn't blow-dry, tightened a bathrobe about her and gazed at the unpromising image in the mirror, which flickered with the candle that she had stuck on the washbasin. Her phone chimed and she walked over to it wearing the oversized fluffy slippers that her grandmother had given her.

Her first signing appointment for the day had cancelled. Not a problem. She only needed two more and her diary was full right up to Christmas Eve. Still, she wasn't taking any chances. She sent a reconfirm request to the next on her list, which wasn't until eleven forty-five, and received an affirmative chime almost straightaway.

That left her with more than three hours to fill in an apartment with a stony chill. Like most people's, Anja's home was all-electric and now there were no cooking options, no light, no heating. She couldn't vacuum, but she could at least dust and polish, soak underwear and wrap presents. The silver brooch for her mum had been a bit extravagant, but Osa only ever wanted the same bottle of liqueur every year, although this time there would be pink thermal bedsocks to go with it. She was more relieved than wistful that she didn't have any brothers or sisters, nieces and nephews to shop for. Afterwards—and she couldn't put it off—she would go down to the bedsit and start cleaning there.

• • • •

Something was sitting on his chest, breathing in his face.

Barely roused, Yannick panicked and threw it off. It thudded against a hard surface and yowled. Then there was silence. Pitch black and silence. He remembered immediately where he was. He had slept deeply, but he had no notion of how long. It was warm. He couldn't remember the last time he'd been so warm. He was also distinctly cramped. The space where he had lain down and fallen asleep was very narrow, hemming him in on both sides. He was just able to roll over on his right side so as to pull his mobile from his left pocket, where he always kept it: only it wasn't there.

He checked his other trouser pocket, then the capacious pockets of the padded coat, which he still had on, then sat up and patted the dirt floor around him. It wasn't there. Yannick crawled both ways along the tunnel circling his palms over the entire gritty surface but found nothing more than a rubber band and an empty crisp packet.

He stood up and cracked his head against the ceiling and had to sit immediately down again. He didn't see stars, didn't see anything. It just hurt. He now became acutely aware of a sickly hangover and he stayed sitting bent forwards while his head throbbed. He could make out faint, muffled sounds of early-morning activity from the main square overhead. If it *was* early morning. He was finding it hard to think in the dark. The top of his head was very sore and smarted when he tried rubbing it.

He remembered that he had slept with his feet towards the ladder. He raised himself to a half-standing position and crept in that direction, not stopping until his right hand struck the aluminium frame and he was able to stand upright in the shaft beneath the kiosk. He was in no hurry to go up. he just needed to be sure where it was. He couldn't afford to lose that mobile. He'd never get another job without one. It had to be here somewhere, dislodged from his pocket after his descent the previous night. He squatted down and waddled back the way he had come, moving his fingers over the irregular landscape of the tunnel like some painstaking piano player on a rough-hewn keyboard.

He hadn't advanced far in this metronomic performance art when something stopped him in his tracks. Something stronger than himself or his anxiety: the smell of frying bacon. His fingertips kept up a perfunctory exploration but his focus was now straight ahead in the direction that his nose was pointing. Someone was cooking breakfast. All he had eaten yesterday was the edge of a cold pizza. He could come back for the mobile later. Keeping his head lowered like a miner to avoid any low bumps in the tunnel ceiling, he started to move more rapidly along.

· · · ·

The manager of the spice emporium, as aromatically gloomy as her empty store, waited impassively, pen in hand, while Anja ran through the lengthy list of requirements and notifications. As soon as she was done, the woman signed the papers, put her own copies in one of the store's linen bags and unlocked the door for the visibly shivering, slightly built young woman.

"Did you walk here?" she asked. "Be careful, won't you?"

Anja nodded, but her smile trembled a little. She set off down the street that had taken her nearly an hour to reach over slippery snow and ice, waiting until she was around a corner and out of sight before tugging a red woollen hat from her coat pocket and pulling it over her head.

It wasn't Tuesday, but she was going to her mother's. She would have to walk there, too. There was no sign of power being restored. Official assurances that normal service would be resumed with minimum delay were being questioned with growing alarm by the limited media that still operated. An accident or problem at the nuclear plant was categorically denied, but no explanation for the outage had been offered, either.

She passed a small group of men on a street corner.

"You shouldn't be out walking alone," said one of them, flicking his red-ended cigarette into the gutter.

She treated the comment with the silent contempt it deserved. It was daytime, or what passed for day in the crepuscular northern winter, and she was free to go wherever she wished in her own city.

Anja didn't like it. The streets were strange, almost deserted. There was almost no movement, the vehicles stationary and hardly anyone venturing out. A single bird flying across her path made her look up, otherwise she kept her head down and trudged determinedly on. This was nonsense. It would all be over quickly and then it would be Christmas.

When she got there, the apartment was in chaos. In a living room filled with dust and smoke, Anastasia and Granma Osa were arguing about a chair.

"It's my chair."

"They *were* your chairs. You gave them to Zachary and me with the rest of the things when you went off to live on your own all the way out in the sticks."

"Mamma, what happened?"

"Your grandmother happened. I suppose I should be grateful she didn't bring a pig."

"A pig is a clean animal," said Osa.

Anja hugged herself. It was sensibly warmer than her own place or the emporium, but she herself was frozen.

Her mother saw her. "Come in, dear, and sit by the fire. The smoke will clear in a minute. A bird's nest was stuck in the chimney and we only just got it out with your old hockey stick."

To Anja's frantic look around the room, her mother said: "Don't worry, I put it back. We didn't burn it."

The furniture discussion was adjourned and the three women positioned themselves, shifting their behinds, until they were shoulder to shoulder on the red leather sofa, now covered with an old sheet and shoved as close to the fireplace as it safely could be. Anja turned and held her grandmother in a fond embrace. The fire was a good one, flames licking the curved back of the tall hearth, but there was no more firewood. Hence the wrangle over the dining room chairs, which could break out again at any moment.

For now, Anja was just pleased to be with her family. If the men weren't dead or otherwise absent, that would be better, but this would do.

Granma Osa had arrived the previous afternoon, when transportation into and across the city was still functioning. When the lights went out shortly after five, she had reminisced with Anja's mother by candlelight and when the chill grew too intense, headed for bed and an early night. By mid-morning, refusing to cower and suffer in the cold, and grumpy from lack of porridge, Osa had said:

"Anastasia, where are your hammers?"

"Hammers? I have one, for putting up pictures. What do you want it for?"

To Anja's mother's galling embarrassment, Osa had banged on neighbours' doors until she had the loan of a club hammer, which she put down on the floor in the unused living room, the handle sticking up, and pulled open the shutters to let in the meagre gleam of the outside world. The room was neatly ordered, if somewhat forgotten, its furnishings perfectly comfortable. It just needed living in. Osa inspected the wall beneath the mantelpiece and flexed her shoulders. She was a short but tough eighty-two year-old.

"There's just a line of bricks there. The chimney's clear and the hearth was a deep one. It drew well."

"What are you...? No, mum, no! You can't."

"No such word as 'can't,'" said Anastasia's mother. She wielded the hammer and struck and struck. Bits of plaster and brick went flying and dust filled the air with every reverberation. Her daughter knew better than to try to stop her now. Anastasia looked on with horror, dismay and a certain illicit delight as Osa leaned into her task. Defenceless against such a resolute assault, the wall sagged and collapsed inwards. When Osa took a rest between swings of the hammer, Anja's mother snatched a picture from the wall above the mantelpiece, a reproduction of a Picasso minotaur, before it came tumbling down with everything else. Whack, whack, thud and the false wall under the old chimney breast fell to bits. After pulling out a couple of loose half-bricks and tapping back the edges, the old woman called it done. She stepped into the rediscovered fireplace amongst the rubble and stuck her hand up the chimney flue.

"Who's going to clean all this up? The whole house is filthy," fretted Anastasia.

Granma Osa eyed her keenly, panting from the exertion. "I'm going out," she said. "I've got my own key."

Anja's mother watched from the second floor window as the unmistakeable, busy figure made a beeline for a parked trailer. Next to it, under ripped plastic waterproofing that had once held sacks of cement, lay a small pallet. Granma Osa lifted up the pinewood platform, sliding off the dusty wrapping, and marched back with it to the front door of the building.

It was the pallet, broken up by the heavy hammer, that now burned so brightly. Smoke was disappearing fast up the cleared chimney. Anja rubbed her nose: it was coming back to life. The women sat and stared at the burning flames.

"What's going on, Anja?"

She had never heard mother ask for truth quite so gently before.

"I don't know," she answered.

She'd seen the newsfeeds and social media. There was growing talk of a nuclear meltdown. There was all kinds of talk. But the bird that she had seen in the street had flown up and away, not dropped down dead. And this wasn't Russia. They wouldn't cover it up. Would they?

"Let's see what they're saying."

She called up on her mobile the most recent item. It was a video, a joint statement to the press by the city's mayor and the Minister for the Interior, recorded just half an hour previously. Above the mantelpiece where the picture had been was a clear, blank rectangle and Anja projected the video there so that they could all watch it.

*

To the urgently called questions, the mayor held up his hands. "First and foremost, there is no cause for alarm. Above all, let me assure you all that there has been no incident at the nuclear plant serving the city. Any rumours to the contrary have no foundation in fact whatsoever."

"So what has happened?" The reporter for a foreign news channel got in there before anyone else. Cameras flashed and the rumble of petrol generators could be heard in the background.

"City council is working closely with national government to get to the root of the problem and solve it in the shortest possible time."

The mayor pointed to a journalist from a newspaper that supported his party and who he might trust to go easy on him. He soon regretted it.

"You say there has been no incident, but there have been reports of unusual activity at the nuclear plant. What can you tell us about that?"

"I cannot comment on—"

When the mayor, deluged by shouts and demands for information, asked for silence, the Minister indicated that he would take the question.

"The integrity and efficient functioning of the reactor and power station have never been demonstrated to be in better order than during the past twenty-four hours," he said. "There has been no accident and no incident at the plant, which is operating one hundred per cent normally. I can tell you, however, that in the interest of the utmost safety and security, the plant has carried out a staged shutdown of activity so that it is now at near-zero productivity. It's safe and it's cold."

"There you have it!" came a shout from the back.

"Why close it down? Minister? Why?"

"Staged reduction of output is the normal and necessary response to a reduction in demand. The effective shutdown is a reflection of that."

"Are you saying there's no demand for electricity? In the entire capital? In winter?"

"That's what we're looking into right now. I know it doesn't make much sense, but it's what the power station is experiencing."

"There's clearly something seriously wrong. Can you rule out a terrorist attack?" asked a right-wing TV station.

"There is no evidence of any attack—"

"But it's possible. That this is terrorists? Could this be a radical Islamic attack on Christmas?

"Until we have more information..."

*

Anja closed off the transmission and the room went dark. The fire had died down.

"About that chair," said Granma Osa.

"Oh, you can have it," said Anja's mother crossly. She turned to her daughter. "Terrorists? Really?"

"We don't know that. But wasn't that strange what he said? That there was no demand for electricity? As if people in the city had no use for it all of a sudden. How long does he think we'll survive without it?"

"We'll need a saw," said her grandmother.

Anastasia was worried and wanted her daughter to stay the night, but Anja couldn't possibly sleep in an apartment with all that dust and mess. At some point during these last two days before Christmas the lights had to come back on, and on Christmas Eve, Anja said, she would bring cured cod and a boiled ham with mustard as long as Osa promised to make her famous rice pudding with almonds and cherry sauce. Osa assented with a pleased nod and Anja left for home fortified by a bowl of porridge that Anastasia had cooked in a pot on the replenished fire. Her mother was getting used to farmhouse life before she even left the city, Anja thought. But thinking also: this was deplorable. It shouldn't be happening.

. . . .

The dull day had faded to near dark already and she walked quickly, without quite breaking into a run. When she reached her building, the continued failure of the security spotlight felt almost like a personal affront. The steps were still gritted against the ice, but Anja was vexed that her exemplary adherence to health-and-safety practice was as nothing in this breakdown of order and all that was right. Yannick hadn't been back. She had thought that he might come by while she was out and need more clothing, but the black bin bag that she had stuffed his clothes and shoes into was still where she'd left it, outside the front door of the bedsit. She'd put his mini-tree and books and DVDs in her own apartment for safekeeping, next to the wrapped presents, where they looked like opened ones. The studio apartment was clean and ready for the next paying occupant.

Anja found her mail in the dark and carried it upstairs, finding the keyhole to her apartment and pushing the door closed with her bottom. She lit the stub of a candle that she had brought with her, setting it down carefully on the hardwood floor, and took careful steps along a hallway hung with boughs of holly. She felt like a stranger, an intruder. Her living room greeted her with silence. Without bright lights and online company, or music, or TV, her home wasn't her own. She couldn't cook or iron or chat with people she knew. She daren't use her mobile unnecessarily because it couldn't be recharged and so what was she supposed to do? Sit in the dark until bedtime? What was she going to do tomorrow and the next day? All her remaining pre-Christmas appointments had either cancelled or rescheduled until the New Year. She could never have gotten to them anyway. It left her one contract short of her quota and no quota meant no salary, which meant insufficient funds for the mortgage payment on the basement studio. There was today's paperwork to do, but she couldn't concentrate on that right now.

She went to the living room window, pulled up the shutter and stayed looking out. She couldn't be sure, but on the other side of the road she thought she could make out at least two faces in other apartment windows doing the same as her, not knowing what to do. She thought of making one call, to Julian, but then remembered that this was his "mindfulness day." Well, she would join him, then. It was a healthy, timely thing to do and she would be participating with him in a spirit of solidarity. She fetched the quilt from the bed and wrapped herself in it on the sofa, tucked her feet in and lit a new candle, a fat gold one that she had been using for decoration, on a saucer on the glass-topped table in front of her.

After several minutes of staring intently and aiming at equanimity, Anja suspected that she wasn't doing it right, because all she felt was boredom underpinned by an inexplicable sense of rage. Unfortunately, she couldn't check online for how to correct it. Freeing her legs, she undid her simulacrum of a blonde Buddha in order to open her packages and mail instead. There was the nutcracker she had ordered; a tea towel with a picture of Einstein sticking his tongue out, which was a Christmas present for her friend Hedwig; five greetings cards in envelopes of different colours and sizes; an invitation for a free first check-up at a fully automated interactive dental clinic; and a creased, already used, scratch card.

The cards were all from friends and Anja wondered why there was never time for friends now, when there always used to be. She would wrap the tea towel and order it delivered tomorrow. But that would mean having to use up the mobile battery—and were the riders operating? She hadn't seen one all day. Their systems would be down like everyone else's. She would get it ready anyway, and throw out the publicity and random trash. The card had something written on it in ill-shaped letters.

What IOU. Y.

Anja picked it up and held it under the candle, turning it over to view the printed result that Y's fingernail had scratched and revealed. She was looking at a winning ticket for a goodly sum of money. One of those you could buy on the street without any ID, so it belonged to whoever had it. Was this for real or was it a joke? It had to be Yannick. She didn't know any other Y's. If it was him, then it wouldn't be a mean joke, but it might be a poor attempt at one. She didn't know him that well.

The apartment was perfectly clean, but Anja felt the need to give it the once over. She retrieved the suite of cleaning materials from under the kitchen sink and rolled up her sleeves. She would get on her knees and dust and wax the wood floor. The windows and mirrors and glass-top table could always use a polish, the taps as well, scrub the toilet and afterwards there would be her nails to do. It irked her exceedingly that she could not launder the sheets and towels, but housecleaning on its own could, she knew, keep her occupied indefinitely. By the light of the gold candle, which she continuously pushed and relocated, she went fixedly and painstakingly about her tasks, until not even she could do anymore and she fell into her bed and lay still.

The extinguished world outside her window, which she had managed by means of her stubborn exertions to block out, sounded a mournful note. The wind was picking up. Her ear followed its harsh, scrappy blowing and kept following it, as if by her attention she could persuade it from cranking up, getting mean. She lay awake, longing herself to sleep, so that tomorrow she would wake to a lamp left on somewhere, the hum of the fridge and the sound of water clanking through the radiators as they started to warm up, but the wind wasn't having any of it. It had decided that it was as angry as she was silent. It wanted to shake her building and went about it with a vengeance. The bedroom shutter that was stuck halfway down shook and rattled in concert with the street's roar and occasional banging. At a certain nameless hour, the moon pulled overhead as if attracted by the racket and wanting to know what on earth was going on. It sent a wakefulness of light filtering through Anja's window. When she turned in her bed in search of sleep and made the mistake of opening her eyes, the moon took it as a cue to speak to her. *Oh, will you look at that?*, it exclaimed like a scandalized neighbour. *Scandalous. Such a din. I think it's getting worse.* The fluorescent hands on her retro bedside clock pointed this way and that and at one point she thought she heard a horse galloping down the street.

At five fifteen the alarm went off. Anja dealt with it. Wind still buffeted the shutter as she lay there, breathing shallowly, and there was rain falling. She licked her dry lips and swung her legs out of bed. She didn't try to hide her ill-humour from herself. The power hadn't returned and somehow she had known that it wouldn't. By the light of the last candle in the apartment, she washed her face and armpits, drips of water running cold down her side until she hastily rubbed them off with a towel. She put on her running gear and drank back a can of fruit juice before blowing out the candle in the hallway and descending the apartment block's interior stairs. She pulled open the outside door and had to close it at once.

It was utterly foul out there, the wind delinquent, violent, hurling icy rain around a dangerously unlit road. To go out in such conditions would be insane. Anja was shut inside with defeat. Hedwig had said that hell would freeze over before Anja missed her morning run and it might as well have done. Then she opened the door and went out anyway to the top of the outdoor staircase, challenging the light to come on. It didn't. With the aid of Julian's headlamp she grabbed a balustrade and took the steps down sideways, her back to the insolent wind. When she turned at the street she had to walk against a freezing spray that stung her eyes and skin. From there it was down blind steps as far as the bedsit and past that to the wall where the binbag of clothes had been shoved, partly obscured by leaves. When she picked it up, it was stiff with frost. She was freezing after less than two minutes outside.

She bustled back up to her apartment, dropping the bag under the coat rack and emitting a shout like an animal. Her body pleaded for a source of warmth and there was none. It ran her yelping back to the bedroom where she dove back under the duvet.

It was a bad situation. With no hot water she couldn't possibly shower again and without showering she couldn't envisage facing the day. She would have to go out and engage with people unwashed. Also, since she disliked cooking, preferring to have ready meals delivered fresh, there was almost nothing to eat in the kitchen, just an apple and a couple of granola bars which she had saved for after her run. As soon as the shops opened, she would go to the supermarket and then the hardware store for camping gas canisters and go straight to her mother's. Around three-thirty that night, when she had been wondering how many chairs Mamma and Osa had left, maybe none, and the table wouldn't be so easy to saw up, she had remembered the camping stove in her hallway cupboard. She would take it with as much food as she could carry. They could cook on it and it would give some heat. Anja pulled the quilt over her head, resolved to wait. There was nothing else she could do.

• • • •

Yannick had entered a different physical space. His right hand, which he had been sliding along the rock ceiling, was waving in space and he could now stand at full height.

"Hallo?" he said.

He heard the rustle of nylon outdoor clothing and then his arms were pinned behind his back and somebody's hands were running over his face and head.

"Who is this? How did he get in?"

"Dunno. Breath stinks. Must be one of the homeless pissheads."

Yannick found himself being pushed down onto a wooden bench.

"Who are you? How did you get in here? How did you find us?" demanded a older male voice.

"There was this trapdoor in a kiosk. I just went down. Then I fell asleep. What is this?"

"And what were you doing in the kiosk? Trying it for the cash, were you? Robbing the disabled? Arsewipe."

"I was freezing. You know what it's like out there. The police were going to get me so I went down the hole. But I didn't do anything wrong."

"Oh, never heard that one before, have you?" the man asked the surroundings.

"Oh, no," said one.

"Not me, either," said another.

"Victim of circumstance. "

"Just a rabbit down a hole."

"Look, I'll just go back," tried Yannick.

"What do you know about us?"

"I don't understand."

"Who else is with you?"

"No one. Look, is that bacon? It's just that I'm really hungry..."

"He's just a lost twat," said the older man with the blunt voice. "Give him something to eat. He'll have to keep us company."

Yannick was handed a plate. He wanted to know what was on it, but it seemed uncivil and ill-advised to ask. By smelling and feeling it with his fingers, he identified it as bread and soft cheese. Relieved, he began eating immediately. The situation no longer seemed quite so threatening.

"Coffee. Hold your hand out." He took the tin mug by its proffered handle and took a taste. It was sweet and strong.

He sensed more bodies moving by. These ones didn't ask or say anything, but he felt individual shock waves from each one, as if they knew that he was there and were making an intense scan of him as they went past.

"Plate and cup: give'em here."

The unfinished cup was pulled from his lips and taken from him.

"Who is our guest?" asked the older man. He had a voice that sounded oddly familiar.

"Pisshead, he's talking to you."

"Me?"

"You. Start speaking."

"My name's Yannick."

"Hallo Yannick."

"Hi Yannick."

"Tell us all about you, Yannick."

Different voices, working as a team.

"Yesterday I lost my job and my apartment."

"Poor Yannick!"

"Lost his job and his house."

"What about the girl? Did you lose the girl, too?"

"I don't have a girlfriend."

"But do you love her?"

There was a silence.

"So what are you going to do about it?"

"Yannick?"

"What can I do?"

It might have been a conversation with himself.

"Cheer up?"

"I'm OK, really. One of the shelters will take me in. I really appreciate you guys. I had better get up and get going."

"Where will you go? You'll stay with us a bit longer," said a melodious male voice.

"You're no bother. It's nice to have a chat with someone new," said a woman.

"You've been very kind already. But I need to go and look for my mobile."

Yannick stood up and was immediately pulled down again by the two men sitting either side of him on the hard bench.

"You're not really going to be missed, are you?" the older voice took over again. "Homeless. On your own. In any case, the police and emergency services are rather busy up top. Overwhelmed, I'm told. They've never not seen anything like it!" he laughed. "There are four tunnels leading off from here. They quickly divide into others and then branch off again. Do you know which one was yours? You had to turn first—or was it second?—right. And then left. Did you count the steps? Then right again somewhere. Do you remember?"

Yannick swallowed. "Who are you? What are you...?"

"Who are we? The homeless pisshead wants to know who we are."

"And what we're doing."

"Nice of him to take an interest."

The chorus of voices again.

"Ask yourself who we are." The older man's tone had a clarity of strength that filled the underground den. "You know you don't belong here with us. What rather obvious fact tells you that?"

"You're not bothered by the dark."

"So you know who we are. We are blind to your sight. Black to your white. We are people."

• • • •

Anja woke suffocating. She flung off the quilt and gasped in utterly dark, stone cold air. Quickly, she checked the clock. It was nine-thirty. Her heart sweat in anxiety at waking so late. She'd slept for over two hours.

She relit the last candle and got dressed in as many clothes as she could put on. Over two long-sleeved tops and the new yellow sweater went her Fair Isle jumper and a long beige coat and her skiing parka on top of all that. Another layer and she wouldn't have been able to move her arms, which already stuck out making her look like a fat doll. Anja tried not to think about it. She stuffed clean underwear, socks, slippers, toiletry bag, Christmas presents and nightgown into a small backpack, strapped it on and poured milk on some muesli, which she chewed joylessly. Without coffee, it was a poor meal. Anja listened. She could hear her own breathing. The wind had died away and there were no sounds coming from street or building. It was utterly still. The other occupants were either subdued and anxious like herself, or gone, or worse.

There no messages on her mobile, which had two bars of battery left. She stashed it with the charger into a pocket of the parka, tightened Julian's headlamp to her forehead and pulled her red woolly hat down over her ears. She snuffed the candle, put on her mittens and wheeled her shopping trolley out of the apartment,

None of her overdressing could insulate her lungs against the arctic air outside. It was horribly cold. This wasn't a lull, it was the invisible victor at work, imposing pain in the body of a city already under its dark thumb If the wind didn't blow, it was because it didn't have to. Anja pulled the empty trolley down behind her in the motionless gloom, hard step by hard step, her breaths coming short and stiff. Her eyes watered and her lungs and face hurt. She knew that if she could see the street, it would be implacable greyness. This was winter, raw and brutal.

All the more surprising, then, to hear people out as she dragged, hunched over, the few blocks to the shops. Individuals scurrying. Men and boys standing by a bonfire they had lit, burning cardboard and old tyres, making it seem more like the deep of night than oncoming day. An old lady wearing double dressing gowns and bare legs was shouting at the chemist's shop opposite the supermarket. "You have no right. I will report you," she wailed. The pharmacist who had refused her prescription stayed inside. Precaution was in the air. The supermarket was only serving people through a barred window and there was a long queue, so Anja went first to the hardware store. It had an old-fashioned bell that jingled as she went in. The store owner, a strong old man, smiled. A kerosene lamp burned in what seemed like a treasure cave.

"Good day, " she wished the owner. "Give me camping gas."

"You have cash, right?" said the man.

"No," Anja shook her head. She didn't have any at home, either. One just didn't anymore.

"Paper money only. Or have you got something?" His look was a coarse one.

Flustered, she turned and toddled her enlarged self out of the shop as loftily as she could. At the supermarket window, she could see that the transactions being conducted in cash also. Clearly, it was going to be the same story everywhere.

Anja held her mobile in a mitten and instructed it to call Julian. They weren't supposed to see each other for another four days, but she needed help. "Voice call only," she told the device. He couldn't see her looking like a Russian doll. A vagrant iciness coated her skin like a crust. "Hi!" she began, before Julian's voice recording cut in to wish his caller a very happy Christmas and the line went dead. Anja sighed in relief. She had not had to admit failure. She smiled and her eyes pooled with tears. She blinked. Something was different. She blinked again. The sallow day was coming on. She could begin to see outlines.

She went back into the hardware store. It was warm in there.

"The trolley," she said. "It's a good one."

"Two gas canisters," he said.

"I need four. And batteries, candles, matches."

"You can have it all and keep the trolley. Just give me a nice kiss."

"Fuck you!" she spat.

The man lolled his tongue out.

After she had slammed the door closed, the bell jangling indignantly, Anja stared at the ghostly world assuming form before her. Did that just happen? Did she really say "fuck"? She never, ever, did that. She walked away, gripping her trolley handle defiantly, as far as a lamppost where she stopped and bit her lip, breathing heavily, thinking.

She undid the zipper on her parka and dug inside a pocket of the beige felt coat underneath. There was just enough dawn dimness to read the print on the bent scratch card that she pulled out. It probably wouldn't work, either, but if it did, that was a lot of cash. The back of the card was stamped with the ID number and location of the issuing office in the central square. She would go there. She supposed she could redeem it at any of the kiosks but couldn't for the life of her remember where she had seen one, let alone know which streets they were on. Afterwards she would go to Mamma and Granma Osa, with or without a trolley-full of supplies. Right now she wanted to win something, or at least to try. She put the lottery ticket back, put her head in its red woollen hat down and got going.

As she neared the centre, Anja wasn't sure if she felt the city's edginess or her own. There was the sound of something tall crashing down and she clung to the handle of the trolley as if to a talisman affording her protection. She crossed the road when she saw that the window of a sportswear outlet had been smashed and the store ransacked. She crossed again to avoid a recycling bin for plastics that had been set on fire and was billowing with acrid smoke. Next to it, a man was shouting up at a window, angry or drunk or both. No one was answering. Only a hound howled from a nearby balcony. A woman out walking another dog, a small terrier, pulled on its lead as it scrambled to get home.

On the next block, something bad came her way. A smiling man in his thirties, walking jauntily. "Hey!" he said as he approached and moved into her path. "Have you got any money?" he said. "No, have you? I need some," she startled herself with own fierceness. The man sneered scornfully, but slunk off to try someone else.

When she reached the great southern square, where the old town began to slope down to the harbour and the sea, she found the perimeter cordoned off by police. They had set up a checkpoint and were only letting through people on legitimate business. She could see the kiosk, not far from the Yule tree under which, in normal circumstances, she would have been singing that evening. She could hardly say she was going there to practise. Shopping was no excuse, either. All the stores for fashion, IT, waffles, souvenirs, the shoe shops and opticians were closed and shuttered. The kiosk would be, too, in all probability, but having got this far...

"ID," the policewoman said before she could open her mouth. "Open the trolley, please."

She checked the empty trolley and took Anja's ID card, shining a flashlight in her face.

"What is your business?"

If I say I'm going to the lottery kiosk, she'll say no, thought Anja.

"I'm going to the cathedral."

"Cathedral's closed."

"I have to pray. Outside the door is also holy."

The officer thought about it. "Then pray for us all," she relented and handed Anja back her ID.

A faint light from the sky glistened on the open square as her footsteps hurried a rhythm to the trolley's wheels. With so few people being allowed in, it felt like she had just received a backstage pass to some momentous event. She had just lied.

Earlier she had said fuck to a store owner. There was no one anywhere near her. Any activity was restricted to a blockade of armoured vehicles and flak-jacketed police over on the far side, around the Town Hall and government edifices. They seemed less than interested in the rest of the broad expanse or innocents abroad like herself. High unmarked trucks were banked against the Town Hall and above them, in the higher floors, windows shone brightly in the ornate façade as if they were the silver coin of the realm. With the rest of the city shut down en bloc, sullen and abandoned, it was as if the barriers and machine guns were there to deter anyone who might want to steal the light.

Anja went more or less in the direction of the cathedral steps then veered away towards the Yule tree, which lifted its heavy branches, frosty and forgotten, against the cathedral's high stone wall. Before it, like its own plucky little sentinel, stood the lottery ticket kiosk, and in front of that was a bench against which a bicycle rested. She recognized its black-and-white chequers immediately, having seen it carried up and down the basement studio steps often enough. She took out her mobile and sent a call to her ex-tenant. There was a very faint ringing that matched the vibration on her phone. She looked around on the ground, by the bicycle, under the bench. There was nothing there. She moved towards the kiosk and the ringing sound became a little more distinct. The pulsing sound seemed to be coming from beneath her feet. She crouched down and put her ear to the icy slab. There it was, unmistakeably. But how?

She cut off the call and got back to her feet. There was no drain it could have fallen down if dropped, no metal grille it could have slipped through, just an even spread of paving. Aware that her battery was almost exhausted, she called very briefly once more. It was as if one of the flagstones glowed with a warm beat when the phone rang. She ended the call. If his mobile was buried—buried where it was highly unlikely to be found—then where was he? The sequestered phone, the ownerless bike and the lottery kiosk made a curious Yannickian triangle that she could not fathom.

She thought of the old war film they had watched, only this time Yannick was the submarine. The square would be his deck, the bike a lifebuoy on a capstan and the lottery kiosk his periscope. As was to be expected, the kiosk was closed, and there was no phone number posted on it that she could call, but the window wasn't boarded up. She stood on tiptoe and peered inside. A tall stool lay tilted against the wall, apparently pushed there by the metal door of a hatchway in the floor. Next to the open hatch was what looked like a rider's delivery pouch.

Anja breathed in the rough winter through her nostrils and steamed it out through the funnels of her battleship. Here was something to salvage or solve. She circled around to the kiosk's steel door and saw that it was not properly shut. There was no one else in the vicinity and the police's attention was elsewhere. She pushed, and the door gave, but the stool was blocking it. She shoved harder and the stool clattered to the floor, slamming the hatchway closed. Anja froze. In the overall silence, the noise had been absolute. She waited, counting the seconds. When nobody came over to arrest her and lead her away, she trusted to luck, stole inside and shut the door behind her.

She struggled out of her backpack, got on her knees and pulled off the mittens in order to get her fingers underneath the steel plate in the floor. She yanked it up and peered in. The opening went down. Well, so would she. She would find out. She inserted her legs in the hatchway, jumped and immediately got stuck. Her expanded self in its multiple layers of clothing would not pass through. Her arms waved and her legs kicked uselessly in the air until one boot found purchase on a ladder rung and she was able to push herself up and out again into the kiosk's cramped box.

Anja told herself to calm down.

She unzipped the skiing parka and slipped it off, transferring her mobile to a pocket in the long felt coat underneath. Even though she was still big, without the bulky anorak she was able to move much better and found that she could just fit through the aperture, which immediately opened into a wider shaft. She went down determinedly, foot by foot, gripping the ladder as if she were saving it from falling and not vice versa. When she reached the last rung, she hung from the ladder and waved her feet around until a toe scraped the floor of wherever she was and she could allow herself to drop gently down.

She illuminated her mobile screen and turned all the way around. The shaft served a crude, narrow tunnel that hadn't been roofed. Her device sounded a low battery warning. She risked the briefest of calls and rang off when a distinct answering ring pointed out the direction of the missing phone. Anja pushed the hair back from her face before moving. She wondered at herself. It was completely dark and didn't feel at all safe and yet curiosity had aroused a kind of joy in her.

She imagined herself in a covert operation in which she, the heroine, would get all the credit by going it alone, while her male colleagues stood ineffectually by. At her medal award ceremony, the uniformed commander standing next to her would no longer smile condescendingly but treat her with due and proper respect, leaning over to say...

"You smell nice."

Anja jumped and let out a stream of expletives in old dialect that she had only ever heard her father pronounce. Before his premature death from a heart attack, such language had been principally directed towards the TV news. Anja didn't know she had it in her. The words reverberated down the tunnel. Then silence crept in and with it, fear. The briefly intriguing dark had become unknown threat, dirt and cobwebs, a lurking killer and a banging of blood in her ears.

"You go first," said the man in a more mellifluous tone. "The other way. There are worse things down here than me so stick close and don't run. If you feel the wall with your hands, you'll be alright. I'll tell you when to turn."

"Who are you?" said Anja.

"I," he said proudly, "am the Wolf."

· · · ·

Less than a hundred metres away, a higher level meeting was taking place. From windows on the fourth and top floor of the Town Hall a stark light shone out like a silent alarm.

"It's now a national security issue," the mayor told his chief of police. "Under the direction of the Prime Minister herself. We cooperate but we have no operational authority and quite frankly I'm almost relieved, because I don't know what the fuck's going on."

"We still have no evidence or indications of a terrorist attack," said the senior police commander. "The airport itself is inoperable, but airspace is secured by the military. There's no evidence of an intervention by a foreign power."

"We have no evidence of anything," said the mayor irascibly. "Which is why Government have taken the situation out of our hands. It's been forty-three hours. Nearly two days. The blackout remains total throughout the capital and our engineers have no answer to it. You hear me? You'd think there'd be a solution, costly and laborious maybe, but a solution. No. Nothing. If we don't get the power back very soon, people are going freeze to death. The water supply is interrupted in the two sectors where it needs pumping. Our people are resilient, stoical even, but communications have broken down and we're seeing panic already. Looting. This country has never known looting."

"We're doing what we can, sir, but—"

"The police are overstretched already, yes, I know, but your officers are going to do whatever it takes, Akim. We can't have a breakdown of law and order on top of everything else. We've started to distribute printed flyers to as many homes as possible to reassure people; to direct the elderly and vulnerable to emergency shelters if need be. Other than that, we're at a loss. Banking and commerce are at a standstill. The hospitals can barely function on emergency back-up. This is one of the very few buildings with exceptional auxiliary power. Right before Christmas: accident or design? Who knows? We've nothing to go on."

"But the nuclear plant is safe?"

"I don't know. But apparently, yes. The army has it under control. Not that they could order a radioactive leak to halt its spread if there was one. Look, you should listen to this—sit down, Akim."

The police chief lowered his heavy frame not ungratefully into a chrome chair at the chamber's long and highly polished table. At the other end of the table, ringed by small glasses, was a bottle of aniseed liqueur that tradition demanded be offered to Christmas visitors. The mayor, who remained standing, unscrewed the cap and poured them each a shot glass filled to the rim. Before they could drink it, the overhead lights blinked out. One of the generators in the trucks outside had run out of diesel. Emergency lamps flickered on to lend a warm orange glow to the wood-panelled office, making it seem quite homely and comforting. It showed up the nutty brown paten on the mayor's head, which was bald except for tufts of hair around his ears.

There was a knock at the door and an aide came in.

"The power will be back on in a—"

"Yes, yes, we know. Is that all?"

"There was a petitioner to see you. An old man."

"A what?"

"It is... Christmas, sir."

"Don't they have any idea what's going on?"

"I know, sir. I told him and he's gone. He left his collective's wish list. Made me promise to give it to you personally." The young staffer placed an envelope on the table and withdrew from the room.

It was a time-honoured custom for the mayor to grant one of the city's disadvantaged or worthy groups a wish on the day before Christmas, a practice going back to the days of rule by kings, when the petitioners were poor or sick subjects. It was normally a moment he enjoyed immensely, as he could play at being magnanimous, dispensing yuletide generosity just like the by-gone monarchs. Last year, he had authorized a trip to Milan for the city's youth orchestra. The year before that, a volunteer centre for migrants was awarded the rent-free use of a discontinued sub-post office. That hadn't gone down too well with voters and he had told the Town Clerk to restrict the short list in future to deserving local-born citizens. It was typical, on the day before Christmas Eve when the Town Hall closed and festivities started with singing under the great tree, for there to be a considerable queue of petitioners waiting to be presented and heard, hoping to be chosen. Today, with this one exception, they had understandably kept away. It was from the Association for the Blind, he noted from the envelope. They were generally well-cared for, or used to be before the cuts.

"An hour after the power outage, I received a phone call from the director of the nuclear plant," said the mayor. "This one."

He clicked on a saved call, which started off with what sounded like light-hearted banter in the background until it was shushed and the voice of the man responsible for the safe functioning of the nuclear facility supplying energy to the capital could be heard on the line.

'We just had to slow down the reactor, in a series of steps. It's a standard, safe procedure, but one that we've never had to resort to before.'

'What's wrong?'

'There's nothing wrong, sir. The plant and its technical operations are working perfectly. It's just that there's no consumption in the capital. Over the space of ten minutes, the entire city went off grid, zone by zone. We produce energy to meet demand, which is always very high in winter time and even more so at Christmas. At just after five pm, demand suddenly plummeted to near-zero, so we had turn off the nuclear tap, so to speak. Everything's in order here, sir, but if something of this nature occurs unexpectedly, protocol requires me to alert the Secretary for Energy and City Hall straightaway.'

'Yes, of course. So what happened?'

'Like I said, sir, nothing here. Engineers ought to be checking on all the substations. I would have them sent there first. Needless to say, Mr Mayor, it's highly unusual.'

"There's absolutely no rational explanation. We've checked the substations. They're fine. But what the nuclear plant reports is correct: the power grid registers no demand. It's like a nightmarish joke."

"Like something the Joker might pull off in Batman," suggested the police chief.

The mayor slid the full shot glass across the table to the other man, careful not to spill a drop.

"You know," he said. "Some of our European neighbours believe that our ancestors used to drink from the skulls of their enemies. It's simply not true. They used the horns of domestic cattle for their ale, but that's about all. Our people were simply not so infernal and cruel then and we aren't now. If it really is sabotage, it must be outsiders. And that worries the hell out of me. It's as if a dark force was grinning. Laughing at us. Enjoying the darkness it's left us in."

"Skål."

"Skål," returned the mayor and knocked back his anise. He picked up the envelope the aide had brought in, marked URGENT by its sender, and unfolded the single piece of paper it held under the pale emergency light.

Our demands, it was headed.

Every fully blind person in the city to be offered:

More help in the home

Cataract operation

Brain implant that translates imaging in a way analogous with vision

Self-driving car share

Exemption from lifting dog poo

Benefits no longer dependent on employment training

Intelligent, luminescent stick to negotiate and interact with a developing smart city

OR a fully-trained guide dog

Also: Reading lenses for the partials

Free audio books

Full and legally-binding agreement of the terms in braille

Tagged onto the end in a clumsy hand was a late addition:

Restoration of meal deliveries, PLEASE!

And a column, also handwritten, but neatly and with a different pen:

21 December

S1 17.05

S3 17.05

S5 17.05

S6 17.06
S7 17.06
S8 17.07
S2 17.09
S4 17.15
Light a candle this Christmas

✳

"Look at this, Akim," said the mayor. "You have to admire the audacity. What do you make of the numbers at the end?"

A humming from the street below heralded the return of the overhead lights. Screens along the back wall brightened and devices pinged and flashed. The heavy detective blinked with them a couple of times and leaned over the page.

"If you don't ask, you don't get, I suppose," he said. "It's dated the day of the blackout. As for the rest: five past five was the first outage. And that looks like the order in which the sectors of the city were blacked out. How many people know that?"

He met the eyes of the mayor, who snatched back the piece of paper and stared at it. He called the aide on duty. "The petitioner: the old man. Don't let him leave. Arrest him." The mayor listened to his phone. "Well, send security after him," he ordered. "Detain him. Do it now!"

"He's left the building," he told Akim. "You're the police: get him!"

Minutes passed and the combined security forces reported negatives in all areas. The square had been sealed off and the few civilians within it rounded up, but none of them remotely fit the description of the petitioner and none was recognized by Town Hall staff or the new police guard on the entrance.

The heavy oak doors of the cathedral were closed and would remain so until midnight Mass. The chief had the temple searched anyway, but drew a blank. The sacristan on duty, who was certainly old enough and held for questioning, turned out to be female. The mayor's visitor had been male, white, probably mid-sixties and heavy set. He looked like a regular local, everyone agreed, although presumably blind. He had been amiable and polite when questioned and had walked carefully yet confidently behind his old-fashioned white stick and dark glasses. He had gained access to the outer chambers of the council without being identified: the newly installed facial recognition software was offline, as were the digital ID readers, and the guards had simply waved the blind old man through the Public Entrance after patting him down and pinning a badge on him. The mayor was informed that on exiting the building, the man had smiled and growled: "See you tomorrow."

A helicopter came to hover over the square and the mayor went to the window, wiping away the condensation with an elbow. He watched as searchlights from the helicopter swept the square, revealing empty, open spaces of bitter dampness, armed personnel and their vehicles, the usual street furniture, high surrounding walls on two sides, a continuous police cordon on the other two, and a forlorn Yule tree. There should have been a gathering there under the tree today, singing in the Christ, the light of the world. Instead, the black magician had somehow folded himself into the shadows and disappeared.

• • • •

"I found another one. Another random tourist, right at the bottom of the main square ladder. I thought it was Sven back already. The door of the hut must be open—I'll go now and check on it personally. We're damn fortunate it wasn't the police. Put her next to him." The Wolf's voice was large and rounded like an actor's. "It's alright, I think," said the man who had brought her. "But we'd best wait and see what Sven has to say. Here's her mobile. Anyway, we'll have to keep her here with the homeless pisshead until we're done."

"What's going on? Who are you? I will be missed. They'll report me lost."

"Lost, but not found. Not down here," declared her abductor.

"Anja?"

"Yannick?"

"They know each other," said a woman.

"She's come to rescue him. How romantic!" said another.

"Sit her down," said the Wolf.

"Is it"—she had to ask—"clean?"

"Oh no," the woman said. "We live in the filth and the bat shit caves of the mind. We wear our affliction on our faces like original sin. We do not wash properly and cannot be trusted."

"But it is horrible down here," said a young girl. "I don't like it. It's smelly."

Anja was sat on a bench, next to a presumable Yannick. With so many layers of clothing on it was hard to tell. She had gone from frozen to warm to hot and flustered. For her Nordic soul, such physical proximity in the total dark was oppressively intimate. She resisted a temptation to reach out and touch him.

"Who are these people you are with?" she asked. "What's happening?"

"I'm not with them. And I have no idea."

"How did you end up down here?"

"I lost my job."

"Another one," Anja smiled in the dark. The mixture of alarm and reassurance that she was feeling didn't make any sense. "It doesn't explain why you're here."

"I was about to ask you the same thing. Did you find the ticket? The lottery?"

"Yes."

"It's—"

Real, he was going to say, but Anja was screaming, for real, and the little girl started crying.

"Shut up, woman, or I'll slap you," said the girl's mother. "Come here, Abegael."

"There was a rat. I felt it touch me."

"That was Silky: she's our cat. The rats are mostly gone, thanks to her."

"Oh!" Anja shuddered.

"She's *my* cat," sobbed the girl.

"It was better when we had the dog."

"Kidnapping and illegal detention are very serious crimes," Anja spoke up with as firm a tone as she could manage. She sounded like her father, she realized, after a day in court.

"So is holding the city to ransom," rasped a man softly, as if amused.

"How long to do you plan to keep us here?"

"That's up to the mayor," he said.

"A roll of the dice," said another voice.

"The wheel of fortune," said another.

"One is born rich and pretty, perfectly formed, another a freak, poor and despised," said a woman who Anja pictured immediately as a witch. "White cat or black cat? Which is it? Lucky or unlucky? They say white cats are deaf. Are you white or black-haired, my lovely? Black and white, sounds in the air. Either or."

For a few seconds, nobody spoke. There was just body language, probing and sensing. Anja drew herself in.

"How many of you are there?" she said.

"More than you can see."

"Can't we have a light on?"

"No. And don't try it. We'll know. We have a light detector and an alarm will go off."

"They're blind," Yannick said.

"What?" said Anja.

"What?" mimicked someone.

"What?"

"What?"

"What?"

The word echoed from anonymous voice chambers ranged around the unknowable space.

"All of them?" said Anja.

"All of them," a young man answered for Yannick.

"What is it you want?"

"I want to go to the park and play on the swings," said the young girl.

"A bit of fun. A better life."

"Sven has our full list of demands. He'll be giving it to the mayor about now," said the man with the gently rasping voice, who seemed to breathe his words out.

"Why should the mayor listen to you?" Anja said.

"He'll have to. He'll have to give in before the city descends into chaos."

"The devil—it was you. You did it. Did you?"

"We turned off the star of Bethlehem," said the witch woman.

"Did what?" said Yannick.

"Cut off the electricity. Everywhere," said Anja.

"It's still off?"

"My mother and Granma Osa are in a flat with no heating. The streets are not safe. People are acting... uncivilly. The supermarkets are being emptied and people are breaking shop windows, lighting fires... I need to use the bathroom."

"Me, too," Yannick said. The unexpected news had unsettled his bowels.

"Come with me." said the rasping voice. "Stand up, both of you. I really wouldn't try anything, by the way. If you run, all you'll get is lost. You'll never find a way out, or even back to here. The maze will take you. And we won't come looking for you. It will have saved us the inconvenience."

His enunciation was the more menacing for being so gentle. He took Anja's left hand in what seemed a courteous gesture until she felt a leather belt tugged tight around it.

"I only have a cat. For Christmas I want a Danish–Swedish farmdog. We had a dog but it got lost. What have you got?"

"Give me your potty, Abegael," said the man to the girl.

"Hold hands," he told the visitors.

"Don't lose them," quipped the witch.

· · · ·

He tugged on the belt and led them away, Anja then Yannick, the fingertips of their right hands hooked together. They went slowly around the cave wall, Yannick letting his left hand skim over its rough surface. When the wall ended and his hand waved in the air, he walked into Anja's back, her head knocking into his chest. They had stopped.

"Follow the rope to the Middle," breathed their guide.

In the empty space their hands found a standing stanchion with a rope attached to it at waist height, like those used to channel people in banks or airports. Anja's fingers tightened on Yannick's and they moved along it. The rope stopped at the corresponding stanchion at the other end, beyond which was another blankness into which they moved, presumably the middle.

"Past table and chairs," said the man, placing Anja's hand on a chair back when she kicked one of them.

He walked them across the Middle for some distance to another upright pole, attached to another rope, which guided them to another pole in the same dark, but somewhere else. Neither of them had known such black on black nothingness ever before.

"Mind your heads in the tunnel," murmured their guide.

As they left the pole behind, the acoustics closed in and their shoulders brushed the rough tunnel walls. Yannick, ducking his head again to keep under the low clearance, imagined the man to be bearing the potty before him like an oil lamp. After several turns and a considerable distance, the man halted them and told them to wait. There were crunching sounds and the clang of iron, followed by low thuds. He appeared to be applying himself to the wall, prising out stones.

"You have to squeeze through here," he explained.

Together they scraped through a gap in the wall into another, damper place that echoed and smelled rank. He released the belt from Anja's wrist.

"You can stand all the way up in here. Turn right and keep your hand on the wall until the rock turns to smooth brick. The throne is right there in front of you. Unisex. No standing and peeing, Yan-Yannick: sitting only. There should be a roll of paper within reaching distance. Then feel left for a bucket of water, soap and a towel. I'll be waiting here. Mind your feet don't slip."

As they felt their way along, they heard a splosh of the potty being emptied into what was self-evidently one of the city sewers. It exuded a tolerable farmyard pong. Anja stepped warily, her face screwed up, closing her mind to what she might be treading in, until she bumped into the WC, which was a wooden box with a smooth seat fitted into the top. She positioned herself and took a long piss that they could both hear empty out directly out beneath her.

"We have to get out of here," Anja whispered. Her nails scratched the wooden box. "There's no toilet paper."

Yannick wasn't immediately sure whether the two comments were related, but he was inclined to agree. The initial appeal of warmth and free food had worn off for him some time before, since when he had sunk into a somnolent apathy. Anja's arrival and her discovery of their captors' wild plot had roused him, but he had no clear idea of what to do.

This was another world of puzzles and dead-ends where he didn't belong and couldn't escape from.

"I don't know how," he whispered back.

"Do you think you could find the kiosk?"

"I've thought about it. We might get lucky and pick the right tunnel from their lair. But then there are turns and not necessarily the first one each time. If we get it wrong—well, you heard what he said."

"If we see a chance, we take it, OK?"

"OK."

"Have you got a tissue?"

"Yes," he remembered, realizing what she asking for. He took the packet from his pocket and held it out across an indeterminate boundary of personal space for several seconds until their hands touched.

"Hurry up," called the waiting man.

"I need to go," Yannick reminded her.

From their conspiratorial lavatory, they trudged carefully back to the aperture in the wall. Something like a glimmer of hope hovered between them. It left them quite unprepared for what happened next.

As they approached the exit, a weird sigh rose in the sewer and wafted a horrid breath into their faces. It was followed by a desperate, sucking sound, while breath was drawn in far away and then unleashed. A fast, fetid wind rushed them, carrying the hostile moan of a beast that had been woken. It wavered and wailed, waited to fill its horrible lungs again and then hit them with a second noxious wave, screaming in their ears.

"Come!" said the man, pulling on them, and then they were on the other side and he was replacing the stones in the wall, blocking out the poisonous sound.

Yannick found that he had to sit down to let the stale air of the tunnel revive him.

"What was that?" asked Anja.

Their guide also panted. "Do you want to go back and find out?" he wheezed.

"No."

"Next time, be quicker. We're going."

Yannick got to his feet. He wasn't going to be left behind. He tagged on behind the other two, who were walking already.

Anja felt nauseous. She had a vision of their slithery-speaking guide as a beast. Scaly with wild, bloodshot eyes, his claws long and curved, his tongue like a snake's. All his underground legion were hideous and deformed. Monsters who could not see or be seen. As for what the sewer harboured, she knew not what, but she could guess. Huge, hateful, sadistic, bent on devouring.

"I feel like I've descended into hell," she said.

"Enjoy your stay," hissed their escort.

• • • •

On reentering the central space, a variety of gentler reverberations and distant murmurs told them that the hideout was quite cavernous and also busy, thronged even. When they reached the Middle, the table was occupied. Sven, the older man, was back and telling the others how his visit to the Town Hall had gone. The man who Anja now imagined as a reptilian beast paused to listen in.

"So what happens now?" asked someone.

"We wait. We let him sweat," said Sven.

"What if he didn't get the note?"

"Doesn't matter. I'm going back anyway. If I have to spell it out for him then, I will. But not until tomorrow. For now we wait, and nobody goes up top. Santa is nearly here and he's going to bring us a big sack of presents. Listen up, everyone," he stood up and spoke out loud in a ringing voice. "Clear the table and chairs away from the Middle and block the exits. Let our ceremonies begin."

Anja and Yannick were returned to the same bench location as before, where Anja found her felt coat draped over the long, hard seat. She had taken it off earlier in the lukewarm fug of the underground den and swapped it now to her lap in the manner of someone ready to leave. She yearned to get back to the kiosk, to her backpack with its presents, to her parka and the trolley left outside. To her world.

From their meaningless position on the edge of the cavern, Yannick and Anja heard and felt people go about and scrapes of furniture. "Away from the Middle." "Sit in the ring around the wall," came friendly, advisory calls. "Keep away from the Middle, don't get caught there." Yannick felt unaccountably anxious and got up, but was immediately told to resume his seat. Their bench moved as someone else sat down on it further along.

"Rubbish bags, rubbish bags. Old for new," offered the witch woman, going the round of the wall. "New bags for old," she said.

"I don't have one," Anja said and received one on top of her knees as the witch swept past.

"It goes underneath your seat, for any personal rubbish," said their new neighbour.

"What's happening?" Anja asked her.

"Just go with the flow. Do what the Wolf says and don't open your egg until you're told."

Anja had so many questions that it was difficult to pick on one.

"Who's the Wolf?" she asked.

"He's the chap who directs the event. The master of ceremonies: you know. It'd be chaos otherwise."

But it is chaos, thought Anja. Dark and madness upon the face of the deep.

"Why did you come here?"

Not the first time, Anja jumped. The little girl was standing right in front of her.

"Are you going to be the sacrifice?"

"Abegael," said their neighbour. "You know very well that the sacrifice is chosen by lots. Come and sit with me or other mummy and wait for the sack to come round. Go on."

"Nnnn!" Abegael made the universal sound of a disgruntled child who is only pretending to mind, before running off excitedly.

"Draw your lots, draw your lots! Sack coming round," a man cried. "Make sure you get your lot. Everyone gets one. Anyone not got one? Don't be left empty-handed when the Wolf calls time."

"Put your hand in the sack and take one," their neighbour explained. "But only one."

The sack was shoved in their faces. It was rough and smelled of old hemp. Anja did as she had been instructed and put her arm deep inside, where there nestled a number of the eggs that the woman had mentioned. She pulled one out. It was plastic, like a Kinder, in two halves that could easily be pulled apart. She resisted the temptation to open it.

"Did you get one?" she asked Yannick.

"Yep."

"I'm thirsty," Anja told the woman. It was a relief to come into contact with someone who sounded normal. "Can I get some water?"

"There will be water bottles coming round after the sacrifice and you can have one then. If you're still alive, of course. Sorry, bad joke."

"Time. Open your eggs."

There was no time for Anja to ask what she meant. The Wolf was in charge now, and everyone was suddenly busy with their eggs.

"What is the shape of your hope?" said the Wolf.

The replies came in a clockwise sequence as Wolf made a circuit of them all.

"A ladder."

"An acorn."

"What is the shape of your hope?"

"A plane!"

"A spoon."

"A mouse."

"A paintbrush."

The answers were getting closer.

"A ring."

"A fox," said their woman neighbour.

A hand tapped Anja's head.

Anja had unscrewed the plastic egg and tipped its contents into her palm. It was both round and stubby.

"A whistle."

It was Yannick's turn.

"What is the shape of your hope?" asked the Wolf, the man with the sonorous voice who had captured Anja.

"I don't know what you're talking about," Yannick said.

"What's in your egg?" Anja whispered.

"We are waiting," the Wolf said.

"Nothing," said Yannick.

"Then you have no hope. We have the sacrifice. Come to the Middle."

The bench shifted again as Yannick stood up.

"Don't go," said Anja.

"Sacrifice walking," someone said.

Yannick went round the wall until he found the rope: and the rope pulled him to the Middle, drawing him in.

"What will you give up?" said the Wolf in a voice that boomed.

"I have nothing to give up," Yannick said.

"What is this nothing you speak of?"

"Futility. A waste of life."

"Then you shall give up giving up," said Wolf. "Come to the oldest of the blind. Come to the Old Father. Don't keep him waiting. That's it."

Yannick felt his left hand taken in a limp hold by someone sitting directly beneath him.

"Put your finger in my eye."

A frail voice. Yannick thought he might swoon.

"Put your finger in my eye."

When the Old Father took hold of Yannick's middle finger, he was powerless to resist. He felt it pulled right into the aqueous sludge of the eye and uttered such a cry that Anja, sitting with her back against the wall, put her hands to her head.

"The sacrifice is made!" the Wolf proclaimed to the assembly.

A thundering filled the lair as its denizens pounded the wooden benches around its perimeter.

Anja felt that she must surely break.

The unruly juddering hadn't stopped when it was taken up by a more rhythmic beating on drums. A heavy, primal beat that was joined by gruff, guttural chanting, a twanging of strings and knocking sticks that Anja somehow knew must be human bones. All around her, people got up and began to sway and dance. It was a dark and vengeful air, heavy with blood and stone and death.

"Here he is," said the Witch, bringing someone with her.

He sat down next to her.

"Yannick? Is that you? I thought..."

"Yes, so did I."

He sniffed the bitter stickiness on his middle finger. He had been had. Unless he was quite mistaken, the Old Father's eye had been half a grapefruit. A trick to frighten children, or strangers.

"I'm not sure if this is for real or if they're just playing games," said Yannick.

"Games are very real," said the Witch. "And time is long. Come join the dance."

"I think I will," said Yannick. "I think it will do me some good. Are you coming?"

"No," said Anja. She wanted no part in it. She wanted her Christmas and nothing else, certainly not this Black Mass and its sinister earthiness.

. . . .

The more Yannick danced to the insistent throbbing and clonking, the longer it went on, the more unencumbered he became. He thudded his boots and emotions into the ground, sweat dripping from his nose, and merged with the rhythm, the yes-no, in-out heartbeat of the universe, discords and all. A passing girl handed him a horn with a sweet liquor which he drank and held aloft, dancing on, his heart deeper and higher, all layers of him ending in nothing and nowhere. The girl returned and danced with her back against him, undulating, raising her arms to join her hands behind his neck and pull him into her. She turned and breathed what seemed like fire into him with an explicit kiss then moved on, leaving him to his own thing, until the mesmeric drumming thundered to a halt.

"That's our first number over," called out Sven. "Now for some bingo."

Somewhat bewildered, Yannick meandered until he walked into a rope. When he retraced his steps, it wasn't the one that led back to his own area of bench and he received a series of cajoling insults as he stumbled around the perimeter, twice having to lift his long legs over more ropes, eventually finding Anja and seating himself, exceedingly grateful for the bottle of water that she put in his hands. He nearly choked on it when she tickled him in his ribcage, or so he thought.

"Hee hee, I'm a gnome and I'm allowed to play tricks," said Abegael. "Can I sit between you?"

"Yes, alright," Anja moved over and the little girl climbed up and wiggled her bottom until she was comfortable. She took hold of Anja's arm and snuggled up to her.

"Bingo cards, bingo cards," a teenager pushed them into Yannick's chest, where he took hold of them. He handed one to Anja.

"Are you serious?" she said.

"Let me! I'll help you."

Abegael didn't wait and grabbed both the cards, poring over them with her hands. When Sven started calling the numbers, she rescanned the braille patterns and when one of their numbers was called, she scratched off its marker dot with her thumbnail.

"Are you alright?" Anja wanted to check. "I mean, you don't talk much and—"

"Shush!" Abegael complained.

"I'm going with the flow," Yannick said.

"I can't hear the numbers!"

Anja hoped he wasn't flowing away on a dream of his own making. They had to do this together. Endure. Focus. Get out.

"Yannick, we're still in the submarine."

"Bingo!" came a shout across the sunken base.

"We lost. You keep talking," Abegael said.

"Second number over," announced Sven. "All change. Men and boys to the east, women and girls to the west. No mixing for one hour."

There came the whirring sound of a dial being wound up and then a *tick tick tick*, like an old-fashioned timer for making a cake.

Abegael pulled on Yannick's hand. "You have to change sides. Will you play dominoes with me?"

"Don't you have stay with the women and girls?"

"I'm a Christmas gnome so I can go anywhere."

"Alright."

They went off hand-in-hand, somehow missing all the other moving bodies, to the other side of the cavern, where the girl promptly disappeared and Yannick found himself in the presence of a young man with sharp body odour.

"Detlef," he introduced himself.

"Yannick."

"It's happening."

"What is?"

"Chaos. The end of times. A phoenix will fly in the black dawn."

"And then what?

"Glorious night will give birth to the true man, the true woman."

"How do you figure that?"

"Don't you feel it, little man? In the dripping rock? In your blood?"

"I thought you just had a few demands. You get what you want and the lights go back on."

"Oh, it's bigger than that. The old order is here undermined. It's falling in on itself."

"So you're not just a bunch of blind people."

"We are the hard core. Extreme Underground. Natural law."

"Go away, Detlef, we're playing a game."

Yannick was saved from further acrid portents by the arrival of Abegael with the set of dominoes. Detlef drifted off, but a reek and vision of imminent doom hung in the air.

The girl hopped up onto the bench where she counted out a dozen dominoes between them and shuffled them round with the flat of her hand. Yannick could hear the unmistakeable sound of their clacking together. Abegael drew her share and pushed the rest towards him.

"Have you got double six?"

He examined the little bumps on the surface of his tiles but was none the wiser.

"I don't think so."

"I've got double five. Your go."

The last time Yannick couldn't read the numbers on dominoes, he must have been about two, and then his mother had shown him how to match the colours. The only one he could recognize now was blank like himself, the tabula rasa on which all remained to be made clear.

"You'll have to teach me."

· · · ·

Anja had no idea if Yannick was still on board with her, if they were together on the escape plan—not that they had one—or if he had surrendered to the hypnotic, drumming delirium of this coven and its nightmarish spirits. There was a disturbingly sombre power behind this game-playing: power enough to assault a capital city. If she saw an opening, a chance, she would take it. There was everywhere to run, everywhere to hide, but as Sven had said, nowhere that she might be found. She could risk it. Just go. Head down the tunnels and hope that she might happen upon an exit back to the real world. The fact that she and Yannick hadn't been tied up or bound to the wall left them free to take their chances. It also meant, of course, that their hosts felt confident to let them try, knowing that they would fail, that they would wander forever the corridors of insanity until thirst and hunger brought them to their knees, the stygian labyrinth claimed them and they turned to dust.

"I think these are yours."

It was the amiable woman from further down the bench.

Anja recognized the slippery surface of the skiing parka she had left in the lottery kiosk and felt the weight of her backpack, holding it up by a strap. Osa's bottle of liqueur was still there, then. In one pocket of the coat was her mobile charger. That belonged to a different existence. What she had to do now was live this one. In the other pocket was the crumpled scratch card that had brought her here. She put the things into her long coat and slid the parka underneath her as a cushion.

"Tell your friend we found his mobile. We're looking after it."

"Thanks," she said. She felt rich. She still had the yellow sweater, a thick pullover, the beige coat across her knees, and now she had the backpack with the goodies. "How did you know it was mine?"

"Your smell. Nice smell."

"Look, listen, I really need a shower: how do you get one?"

"I'm afraid you don't. Not until this is resolved. Tomorrow, Sven says."

"My name's Anja. I expect you know that already. What's yours?

"I'm not supposed to say, sorry. I hope you're not offended."

Anja didn't mind at all. It was simpler, in fact. She already had the woman down as Could Almost Be Normal. To go with Witch and the Beast. For them to vanish as oddly as they had appeared, which is what Anja desired, these people had best remain anonymous. Sven was the only named adult and apparently he could not be wished away.

"Because Sven says so? He's what? Your leader? Your Charles Manson?"

"Hardly. More what you would call our guiding light. We wouldn't be here without him."

"You want to be down here?"

"Yes and no. It's not healthy for the girl, but we do go topside more days than not, and she spent most of the summer getting sun on her skin. Some of the partials function very well up there, but it's your world, isn't it? For us, it's one hazard and obstacle after another. We made our own world here, for a while, and not just as a physical space. We've all changed because of it. Anyway, here is everywhere and this is all nearly over."

"What is it that you want? Why are you doing this?"

"Our demands, you mean? Our shopping list? I have a copy of it here. Wait a minute... Right, well, the really interesting ones for me are more help in the home—who doesn't want that?—and the new brain implants. But there's also stuff like car shares so that we can get around cost-free and intelligent sticks that communicate and tell you what's going on and how to get there."

Anja thought about it. "All those things you could get by applying yourself and hard work," she said.

"And what kind of work would that be?"

"Whatever you have to," said Anja. "Business, music, I don't know. You work and you get a reward."

"Businesses don't like taking us on. We're unsightly. There aren't blind blues players anymore, but a few of us make it as a lawyer or a marriage counsellor, or radio presenter. Not many. Most of us are admin fodder, call centre drones, or were before AI came in. Now there are none of those jobs, but they still put obstacles to our access to benefits and the heating allowance was cancelled last year. A lot of us don't trust the world which lies beyond our senses, the one that you see, and with good reason. This is about the only way we were ever going to get your attention."

"But you have the city a war zone, people being robbed and probably freezing to death and starving."

"Whoever's in charge will be keen to strike a deal, then."

"Aren't you afraid of being caught? You'll go to prison."

"Heads we win, tails we lose. It's like the lottery, you see. For some to be born lucky, others must fail."

"I don't believe that," Anja said. "You make your own way, your own fortune."

"Do you really think you're in charge of your life?" the woman asked.

"Of course. What else?" Anja said.

When the woman said nothing, Anja asked, "What are you thinking?"

"About an astronaut in space, drifting off into oblivion after her anchor to the ship breaks during a spacewalk, but she doesn't despair, not for a moment: she believes she is flying off into an adventure of her own making. Do you love him?"

"Who?"

"Who do you think?"

"Oh, he's not my boyfriend. I'm seeing someone. His name's Julian," she said, as if to remind herself.

"He'll be worried about you."

"I don't think so. We're not due to meet until the twenty-seventh."

"You're not seeing him for Christmas?"

Anja didn't really know why not, she realized. Julian had just told her and she hadn't given it another thought.

"He'll be worried alright. It's getting dicey up there. And this Yannick: is he a good'un?"

"He's nice. But always depressed. It's like he's permanently lost."

"At least someone knows which planet he's on."

"Why is everyone here so strange?"

"Isn't it wonderful?" said the woman. "Abegael seems to like him."

"Are you the girl's mother?"

"One of them, yes. My wife will be over in a minute with some fish and sausage."

"I don't—I can't... I can't eat anything." Anja fingers retreated beneath the coat on her lap. She could not touch anything here and there was nothing to grasp.

"It's disgusting," Anja couldn't help saying. "It's vile. This whole place. This prison."

"We keep it as tidy as we can," she heard the woman say, amused. "Prison would be much nicer, of course. Neat and clean, three meals a day, no housework, counselling, a gym, books. No cockroaches or spiders. Or worse."

· · · ·

"I can't go," Yannick said for the umpteenth time. He had just lost to Abegael four times in a row.

"You're playing it wrong. You've got a five. This one. Five and blank."

Yannick could tell no difference on the Braille dominoes between five and three or two, or between and four and six, and had resorted to passing unless he had a blank or a one, which was a single dot.

"I'm six. How old are you?"

"Twenty-five."

"You don't know very much."

"No, I don't."

"I'm bored now. Goodbye."

"Goodbye," Yannick said to the empty space where the girl had been. He carefully swept the dominoes into the cotton bag that they had come in. He shook it once by its draw strings, rattling the wooden tiles, and placed the bag beside him.

"Can you read them? What they say?"

It was Sven. The man was seated close by. Yannick could hear him chewing.

"They're not runes."

"A mind can read any stone," said Sven. "Does two and three mean nothing to you? From something to a greater something? Four and two, a balanced imbalance of equals. Blank and six: Pluto and the Sun. One and one: togetherness."

"Blank is my mind," said Yannick. "What are you eating?"

"A bone with a bit of pork on it. Want one?"

"Yeah."

"Hold out both your hands. Here."

A pork chop thudded into his right hand and a paper serviette was tucked into the left. The chop smelled warm and tasty.

"How did you know where my hands were?"

"How did you know?"

Yannick felt a cap being tugged onto his head.

"How do you know where your head is? Can you feel it? Can you hear it? Can you *see* it?"

"So you're very good at spatial configuration."

"Very good. Beer?"

"Love one."

A can was plonked on the bench next to him.

"Do you visualize it somehow? How does it work?"

"I take it and I put it down."

"How do you know that it's still sitting there? Someone might have walked by and swiped it."

"It's not my beer, is it? Why should I care? Look, Homeless, I picture it, right? In the same brain cortex where you see it, but with none of your light and shadow and colours, or so I'm reliably told. It has size and shape and weight and textures and position. And temperature. Drink it while it's still cold."

"It's a good chop."

"They tell me your girl won't eat anything. Not a sausage."

"Can't you just let her go? You'll still have me."

"Do you have any less stupid questions?"

"Are you going to kill us?"

"That's better. No. Next question," Sven belched. "I wouldn't have wasted a pork chop otherwise."

"How did you make all these tunnels? I don't see how it's possible."

"We didn't. They were already there. Quite a variety of them and all useful, but these ones here are the really good ones. German-made, nineteen-forties, and still in good nick. We discovered that three of our kiosks were stationed directly above one or other of them and all we had to do was dig down."

"And where are we now?"

"The main bunker, which would have been the Nazi command centre."

"I mean: are we under the Town Hall? Under the cathedral?"

"No, we're seven minutes' walk away, under a furniture store. Trying to get your bearings, lad? Don't bother. The maze is full of trickery, and if you take it on, it will take you. From here, the hub, the tunnels snake off, interconnect with each other and run riot. If you know the way, there are two other bunkers, but there's nothing in them, no food or anything. Then there are two nineteenth century escape tunnels with spiral staircases down from the old palace. They both run parallel to the Nazi ones, and so we just had to knock the walls through here and there to link up with them. Same goes for the big sewer. There's also a disused freight train tunnel running four metres below everything else. We dug down to that as well, so there are nice big holes to walk straight into. If you don't break your neck or a leg and can still walk, the freight tunnel comes to an end at iron gates after an hour or so in either direction. The old escape tunnels from the palace are blocked by cave-ins and you definitely do not want to take on the sewer."

"Why?" Yannick's eyes widened. He wanted to hear it.

"Hydrogen sulphide for a start. How would you like to die from rotting egg gas? That comes from decomposing waste and seaweed. It knocks you out and kills you in a matter of minutes. That's not the biggest danger, though: it's rain. This is the last section of the sewer, going downhill to the harbour. Only takes a light rain to have street drains emptying torrents through feeder canals and then the sewer floods. Just after you feel the wind driven before it, a humongous slug of water will hit you and it'll be goodbye amateur explorer. Or would-be escaper."

It was more than enough to explain the urgency with which their guide had pushed them through the WC visit, but Yannick wasn't completely satisfied. He remembered the terrible shrieking they had heard and the hairs on the back of his neck stood up.

"There's something else down there as well, isn't there?"

"You know about that? It's not something we care to talk about."

"Has it attacked anyone?"

"It doesn't have to. It just sucks you in. We lost the dog to it."

"And you still use the sewer?"

"We know how it works. You don't. Hey, why did the blind man bring a piece of sandpaper to the desert?"

"I don't know," said Yannick.

"He thought it was a map. Hahahahaha," the man started laughing and wouldn't stop, which was when Yannick realized.

"I know who you are."

"What?" said Sven.

"You were on a course I did. For budding electricians. Either we did it or we lost our right to benefit. You riled the teacher."

"I did more to her than that. What a woman. You have no idea. Made my hair stand on end like a Van de Graaff generator. You were on that? What a gift that course was. Like a lamp I rubbed and now the cave is about to fill with treasures."

"So you did it: knocked out the electric?"

"With some help, yeah. The main power lines also run straight underneath the streets. We came across one knocking through the tunnel walls, which is not as dangerous as it might sound. They're so heavily armoured and insulated, you'd need an industrial tool to penetrate or break them."

"Which you have," Yannick guessed.

"We acquired five. The city's power grid is zoned into eight sectors. Five main lines control all eight."

"And you just cut them."

"You make it sound very simple. It's really fucking dangerous. When we found a cable, showing it an ordinary NCVT would tell us if it was live by beeping, but we had to use eyes to read a multimeter to know if it was a high current service cable."

"What's an NCVT?"

"Non-contact voltage tester. Didn't you learn anything on that course?"

"No."

"You weren't listening to teacher. It detects the electro-magnetic field generated by a live cable. Anyhows, when we got the five we wanted, it's not like we could flip off a circuit breaker and safely cut the wires. They were always going to be not only energized but carrying a massive current."

"Surely, if you hit a high voltage cable like that it will blow you up?"

"That's where your Heavy Duty Cable Spiker comes in. You clamp it onto the cable, which is a whopping eleven centimetres thick, and then retire to a safe distance. Seven metres is what we had. When you're ready, you pull on the lanyard and a cartridge fires, which drives a steel chisel to sever the cable."

"And it worked."

"Bloody did! We had nasty arc flashes, mind. No one was hurt but if the operators hadn't already been blind, they probably would be now."

"When you said you used eyes..."

"There's one bloke in the lads' band who can see. Confessed pagan, really into the mythic warrior thing, wants to see the mighty fall and a new world rise, or the old world rise again, the which escapes me. Disaffected, you might say. A good welder. He was more into the plan than we were. Band practice was always above ground, in a garage, but we let him down here for the duration. He's our light detector. Don't worry, we keep him blindfolded—"

"Detlef," Yannick forestalled Sven's chortle.

"Have you met him? Sighted Detlef, yeah."

"He wants mayhem. From what he says, it sounds like he's getting his wish. Was that the idea?"

"Yeah, well, hopefully not for much longer. We just want our Christmas presents. You better hope we get them, too, Homeless."

Driiing! the cake timer declared.

"Alright, listen up," Sven got to his feet and bellowed. "One minute, people. Line up, girls. Line up, boys."

Sven sat down again.

"What is it?" said Yannick.

"Third number," said Sven, patting his knee.

. . . .

Anja's hope that Almost Normal might turn out to be plain Normal had been confounded when her wife, who materialized as promised to ply them with a plate of fish and meat snacks, turned out to be the Witch. Anja had shaken her head, wishing the food and the ghoulish image in her mind away, but soon found herself wedged between the two of them. The Witch rocked on what Anja imagined to be a bony bottom, exuding a strong hint of patchouli. Abegael sat on Almost Normal's lap, quiet for once, probably asleep. Other people were still talking, mostly in low voices, rearranging themselves, some huddling together on the long bench, when a woman's voice rang out:

"Where will it take us? Where will it be?"

"Into the whale, under the sea," called back a man from the opposite side of the wide hollow, receiving murmurs of appreciation and approbation from his fellows.

The shuffling sounds stopped and then the whispered exchanges ceased also. Someone coughed and then there was nothing. It was soundless. As far as Anja could tell, the male and female contingents faced each other across the void, like formed ranks of opponents. Nobody moved. A minute passed. Anja listened, all ears, for there was nothing else to be. As the silence grew, she felt her chest rise and fall and a nameless anxiety fill her empty eyes. The silence began to explore, expanding, making itself felt, steadily appropriating the air that filled the chamber until it reached everywhere, prickling her hands and the skin on her face. When finally it tensed the space between her ears and she could bear it no longer, when it was so big as to be loud, it distended once more like an overinflated balloon. Anja closed her eyes and thought of her mother and Granma Osa.

"What is our hope?" called a man.

"A sound in the air," a woman answered swiftly.

"Dead ends," said another.

"A golden calf," said the Witch.

"A stranger."

"A lone tree, far away. Tiny droplets hanging on pine needles."

"The riverbank."

"The promise in our eggs."

The women giggled and shifted on the bench. Anja realized that she had been holding her breath and breathed out, deflating. The tension had been broken.

"How will we be?" asked an old woman.

"Misunderstood," a man answered.

"Fêted and fed," said another.

"Invariably."

"And not just once."

"Turned on a potter's wheel,"

"Eaten by the maze."

"Welcomed by the forest."

"Lost on other ways."

And so it went on, back and forth. A woman or a man sent a challenge across the divide and the other side countered with a jumble of answers. It made no sense, but Anja felt strangely comforted and excited.

"Climb with me to a cedar cabin," began a youth, and the women and girls carried it on with replies.

"Thick with rugs."

"High in the branches."

"Made by the woodpecker."

"Saved from the woodcutter."

"Kettle in the corner."

"Dripping leaves for shelter."

"Singing in the dawn."

"Ooooohh," intoned Almost Normal and the rest of the female company took it up. "Oooooohh, always started!"

"Ooooohhhhh," the men roared back. "Ever begun!"

With which everyone stood up.

"One more each," directed Sven. "A singer, and the last goes first: men and boys."

Yannick was somewhat lightheaded from having risen too quickly. He stood between Sven and the man who spoke in hushed tones, the one Anja called the Breathless Beast, wondering who their singer would be, but neither they nor anyone else in the male line-up said a word. If a group mind determined what transpired in this phantasmagoria, then his choice would be the Wolf.

"Star War."

It was Detlef. The singer's mantle had been claimed and his fellow men resumed their seats.

"Leprous snowman
Kicked dog
Raging spirit
Arrow in the heart
Star war!
Star war!"

Sighted Detlef snarled in leaden, black metal style.

"Iron heart
Fist of earth
Natural ruler's
Double-edged sword.
Star war
Star war
"Slaves of stars will wield it in their hands
Slaves will choose a king for their own land
Old law
Old law
"Rising up
Casting down
Spears from heaven
Forged in a crown
Star war!
Star war!"

"Star war!" chorused a single voice as the gothic offering ended. It was the Old Father, but whether the blind patriarch was being enthusiastic or ironic, Yannick wasn't sure.

He himself felt uncomfortable, embarrassed even, that the men's collective expression should have ended in such a way.

He could sense a shocked silence on the other side of the cavern. A subtle pattern of trust had arisen in the enigmatic conversation between the sexes to tingle with a peculiar life of its own. Detlef's warring song with its fetish for antiquated weaponry had grabbed it and bludgeoned it. There was a disquiet quiet and for some reason Yannick longed for the sound of lightly falling rain.

Heated discussions now started up among the women, which the men took as notice that they could talk, also. A disorderly and disappointing loudness took over. The enquiring, communing spirit of the convocation had fled into the tunnels and there seemed little point in pretending differently

"Perhaps we should wind it up," said Breathless on Yannick's left.

Sven, on his right, said nothing. Instead, he took the bag of dominoes from Yannick's fingers and swung it to strike the other man firmly on the back of his head. When Breathless gasped, Yannick stifled a laugh.

There came sibilant hushing sounds from the women and girls. One of them had stepped forward to answer. The talking fell away and a tentative stillness held again. The woman waited, collecting either herself or the attention of the whole body of people. Sven gave Yannick back the dominoes.

When Anja started singing, Yannick felt a tremor pass right through him. It was clear and strong and she didn't have to search for the words: they were present in her mind from recent choir practices. It was a carol that she should have been singing that evening with friends and their families under the great fir with its coloured lights, in a world that once existed, where darkness was, but only because light was also. To the singer, it felt like a slim sceptre that she held out in defiance of her jailers in this hateful dungeon.

"Bethlehem Down is full of the starlight,
Winds for the spices, and stars for the gold,
Mary for sleep, and for lullaby music,
Songs of a shepherd by Bethlehem fold."

The sympathetic spirit had returned. It had halted its flight through the tunnels when it heard her voice. It had turned and snaked all the way back and into their midst like a genie whose lamp had been rubbed.

"Here He has peace and a short while for dreaming,
Close-huddled oxen to keep Him from cold,
Mary for love, and for lullaby music
Songs of a shepherd by Bethlehem fold."

Anja ended her song.

Sven stood up. "That's it," he said. "Mingle, do what you want. For anyone who's still hungry, there's buffet leftovers on the Middle table. We come together again in the morning, if and when I get back from our temporal rulers."

The Beast and the others stood up and moved off. Yannick couldn't move from the spot. The librarian in him tried to sort the images and impressions of the last hour into categories and make correlations, but nothing came of it. He suspected strongly that the meaning of it all would not yield to normal reasoning and cognition and that only dream logic would tell him what he needed to know. He dipped a hand into the cotton bag and let it roam among the stones, as if searching for a lucky one, trying to understand he knew not what.

"Haircut? Manicure? Haircut? You could do with one."

Yannick swivelled round from side to side as if by doing so he might see who the person behind him was.

"Remember me?" The girl put her hands on his shoulders and wiggled her tummy into the small of his back.

"The dance floor."

"Grooving and grinding. There'll be more sounds now, but not the Ásatrú band, something more dancey. You were a very good sacrifice. That shout was terrific. I got goosepimples."

"I was terrified."

"And I thought: he's nice, so when I bumped into you, I thought I'd give you a rub-up. I don't want sex, though, I have a boyfriend and the sex is just sooo good, but I do like touching you. So do you want a haircut or what? I have my scissors and comb here."

Her scissors went snap snap snap in her hand and a comb tugged back the thick, straggly forelock that fell over his eyes.

"Alright," said Yannick.

The girl ran her fingers through his hair, making his scalp tingle.

"The sense of touch is most acute on the tip of your forefingers and the tip of your tongue. Know what I mean?"

"What's this? The numbers on it?" Yannick took her hand and placed in it the domino that had stuck between his rummaging fingers.

"Double three," she said.

"What does it mean?"

"It means you've got a double three. How short do you want it?"

"Just go ahead," he said. "Do what you want."

. . . .

When her song was finished, Anja stood still and undisturbed for as long as it took Abegael to run over and into her, hugging her legs and not letting go. The other women soon came to fuss around her, Anja stiffening as she was stroked and patted all the way back to her parka-cushioned seat, dragging the girl with her all the way.

"That was so pretty," said an old woman. "I feel we put the men in their place."

"Did you like what we made?" asked Almost Normal. "It reminds us of what we are. A cabin among the birds, hearing the rain. With a pot for coffee."

"But she sees the starlight," said a girl.

"I had a sighted girlfriend once," said the Witch. "She told me it was like pressure on the skin, but weightless, a constant surprise that didn't go away, a wavelength of enchantment like music, sweet as a tumbling stream."

"That's a good thick cotton," said the old woman seating herself at Anja's side and rubbing her trouser. "So nice and smooth. Is it green?"

"Yes," Anja removed the hand. "How did you guess?"

The other women moved away to other conversations and they were left together with Abegael, who balanced herself on the old woman's knee and put a thumb in her mouth.

"It feels green."

"You can feel colours?"

"I can feel some of them. It's in the dyes they use in the fabric, you see, dear. Red's rough or even sticky. Yellow's just slippery. We don't feel colours as such."

"Are you totally blind?"

"So I'm told. I wouldn't know what not blind was. I was born this way. There are apparently a lot of nearly blind who can sense what you call light. And black and white. I wouldn't know anything about that. Sven wouldn't have them down here, or the partials with their seeing aids. Keeps us all equal, he says."

"Don't you miss your home?"

"I do. But this has been so much fun. I usually only come down here to meet people and say hello, but this time, I got stuck in the power cut. It's been a long time and I miss my bed, but it'll be worthwhile: I'm so looking forward to getting the meals back again. And a talking stick."

"Do you know your way out?"

"Of course, dear."

"I need to go to my mum. She's at home with my granma Osa and they won't have anything left to burn. Or food, or anything: would you show me the way?"

"Oh, come, now. You know we can't do that," admonished the old woman. She rapped the hard ground with a stick. "I miss the trains. They used to rumble along so happily beneath us."

What she wouldn't give to be on a Metro train, thought Anja, getting off in her mind's eye at the station nearest to her mum's, running past the colourful extravaganza of its decor and up the escalator, up to the swing doors of the exit to burst free into the air and the light: the city lights and the open air...

"Do tell me about your young man. Have you known him long?"

• • • •

"I do like my hair to feel nice, don't you?"

"Nnnhnhnnn," said Yannick. He wanted the post-coiffure head massage to go on forever, to the soft beat of the deep house music that was playing, but with a final flick of her fingers, she said: "You're good. Go and show that girl your new haircut. Now she's got some hormonal orifices. I get why you want to be around her. Shake off the bits."

He raised his hands to his head. She had cut it right back, but something was left.

"Thanks," he said. "What can I give you?"

"Can I feel your face?"

"Sure."

She ran her hands over the stubbly contours, over his cheekbones and strong jaw and a fingertip around his lips.

"Hmm," she said. "She thinks you're depressed."

"What?"

"We can help you with that. You just need to go out to the forest with my boyfriend and a few of the lads. Somewhere nice and quiet, and they'll beat you up. Always works."

"I think I prefer biking," Yannick said politely, remembering what scant relief his cycling excursions had given him.

"Then there's forest bathing."

He pictured a clearing in the shadow of tall, frosty pines and an icy green pond waiting.

"I don't..." he began, but the nameless girl, like a dream upon waking, was gone.

Yannick felt different, as if relieved of more than just unruly hair and a provocative presence. He stood up and started walking across the stone floor in the direction of where he remembered hearing Anja sing, when his passage was blocked at his thighs by one of the guide ropes which led from the cave's edge inwards. He followed it to the stanchion on the verge of the Middle, the heart of the hub, where there was nobody and nothing, and gave himself over to a waking dream.

Images of branches, gentle rainfall, gold and silver stars. As always, it was night.

The tree cabin was a raised hut on the edge of a tropical forest, where it looked over shadowed sand onto the starlit purple of the ocean. Rain dripped through the fanned-out fronds of an overhanging palm, playing the roof like a glockenspiel. Any drops that fell into the sand were muted, but when a holy white cow passed along the beach below, a brief, heavy shower rebounded from her back in harmonic exuberance. He jumped down from the hut and walked away from the trees and their rain, across a beach of dry sand under a warm night sky. The ocean heaved a long greeting.

Once more he stood in warm shallows at the water's edge and tiny stars dropped out of the blackness to float down, some faster, some slower. And once again, as they melted into the sea, the glints of sparkling silver played simple sounds as they lit up the surrounding wave in blues and greens, oranges, yellows and pinks.

It was the ocean's own song, as much the sea as its saltiness and briny stench, the wetness on his skin, the resistance and the pull, the unified surface, the combing scrape of a receding wave, the buoyancy, the dangers in its immensity. Just as the six blind men in the story knew an elephant to be utterly different according to the particular part that they touched, it was all of these things. What it was not was the word *sea*, a brief sibilant that was already gone.

The tropical hallucination turned in his mind's eye and there was his father, hanging by both hands from a magnolia tree, wearing a short-sleeved shirt emblazoned with colourful macaws, a black patch over one eye and a big smile. If experience is reality, then what is this? Yannick mused. Costa Rica? Did it even exist? Did his father?

His hand took hold of the cold steel stanchion and the reverie was extinguished as the pole earthed him back into the only real story he knew. He was shocked back into the bunker, its dank and its dust, where he and Anja were trapped. This wasn't their party and it wasn't their war. They were in deep trouble. The submarine was running out of air and they had to get to the surface. Suddenly his mind was as galvanized as the post that he gripped like a joystick. His thumb moved over raised bumps on its otherwise smooth top. He circled with his thumb some more, his eyes closed, and saw a pattern. Four dots. It meant something. A code. Information, even if he didn't know what.

Yannick set off in search of another clue and bumped into a teenage boy making his way to the buffet table, who took him to the next stanchion.

"How many posts are there?" Yannick asked him.

"You mean ropes? Four. One for each tunnel."

"Which one leads to the..." said Yannick to the emptiness. Once again, someone had disappeared on him. "WC."

This second post also had a Braille symbol stamped into its cap. He couldn't read it any better than the first one, but he knew that it was different. Three dots, not four. By taking the angle of the rope as his pointer and advancing hunkered down with arms outspread, he managed to hit upon the two remaining posts and confirm his hunch that they, too, bore a symbol that might tell a person where they were. Even if they stopped short of the Middle—the inner field where a table and chairs were typically set up—the ropes strung between the stanchions still neatly divided the round cavern into four quadrants. One for each tunnel, the boy had let on.

So each time the long cave wall ended at an empty space and a post, that gap was the mouth of a tunnel.

He returned to the wall and made his way round the circumference, calling Anja's name. After nearly falling over seated people's feet and getting roundly admonished, he found her on the same bench seat where he had last heard and felt and smelled her.

"Are you on your own?" he asked.

"Yes. Come and sit down."

"Come with me," he said.

She took her hand away from his. "Go away. I mean, I don't want to dance with you. I'm starting to forget what you look like."

"I have an idea," he said. " I want to show you. What are you wearing?"

"Really," she said.

"I mean: are you still wearing a knitted jumper?"

"Yes. And before you ask, it's cream and grey." Anja put her shoulders back instinctively. He wasn't going to ask about what she had on underneath, was he?

"Do you think you could unravel it?"

"Unravel it? My aunt gave it to me. What for? I'm not what's-her-name. Ariadne."

"I think you have to be," Yannick said.

As she listened to a suddenly cogent Yannick, explaining quietly what he had in mind, Anja's incredulity gave way to hope. It was a clumsy plan but she would take it. Better the faintest of chances than none at all and Yannick's idea wasn't all that outlandish. She had almost given up on him. She pulled both woollen jerseys over her head and off, handed him her new yellow sweater, and used her teeth to break a thread and start undoing her favourite Fair Isle.

When they asked to use the WC, they were promptly escorted there by the Wolf, who made clicking sounds with his tongue as he walked, echo locaters that kept him to the centre of the tunnel. He didn't need to use his stick to hit the walls and find his way, but he did so anyway, just to remind them that he had one and keep them keen. He wasn't taking any chances with the sightseers on what was meant to be their victory eve. He turned and they turned behind him, following the medley of sounds he made.

Anja was having great difficulty in keeping up. The large bundle of wool that she was letting out along the floor got tangled twice and she lost two or three metres of wool each time. If she hadn't sacrificed her yellow sweater as well and tied all the wool together, she would have run out long before they reached the point where the tunnel gave access to the sewer.

While the Wolf dislodged the stones to open the gap, she broke her thread and tied the end to a pen from inside her felt coat, jamming it as best she could into a fracture of stone at the foot of the wall.

After making use of the facilities, tiptoeing all the while—the sewer was eerily quiet—they headed back again, this time with their tracker in place. As they went along, Yannick patted down the snaking wool flush to the ground and pushed it against the wall, while Anja attempted woefully to distract their cooperative jailer with conversation. He ignored her completely and carried on clicking, so she gave up. It didn't matter. They got to the cavern without Wolf getting his boots caught up in the twine or feeling something extraneous underfoot.

He led them via the ropes back to their seats and they were able to determine that they were pretty much directly across from their exit. There were more people around, so they could not talk of what they had just done, but they both knew that a guide line to the sewer now led all the way back to the bunker, where it was tied to the stanchion in the mouth of the tunnel: the only one to present just two bumps in its cap.

Neither of them knew what the Braille symbol signified, but they didn't have to. To them, it read: Way Out. When everyone had gone to bed, they would get up at a prearranged signal, find their way back to the sewer's broad passageway and take their chances against its slimy uncertainty, flash flooding, toxic gas and doubtful egress. Not to mention its resident leviathan. Ominous on all said counts, a public utility had to have periodic access points from the surface, Yannick had argued. He was tall enough to encounter any descending step ladder if he walked along with his hands raised. Perhaps, he said, there might even be a glimmer of light from a manhole above if it were day, or electrical light if by some miracle it had been restored.

They sat side by side, hearts beating. All they had to do now was wait, make whatever small talk was necessary, and hope that their subterfuge remained undiscovered. Nobody paid them any attention. If Sven's tactics paid off tomorrow, an improbable victory was within their grasp and the empty hollow would overflow with fulfilled promises like their very own Santa's grotto. Someone strummed a guitar while an excited buzz circulated among the people.

With nothing else to do but pass the time, Anja and Yannick told each other their personal stories. One family driven by success, the other more desultory. A future mapped out and a future hidden in a dream map that could not be read. Her mother a standard-bearer for her late husband's illiberal juristic values, but now somewhat lost. His mother lost forever to the bane of cancer. Both fathers gone. One succumbed to cardiac arrest; another absconded to Central America.

"Which is how I ended up at your place," Yannick said.

"You make it sound like it all happened to you. I think we choose what happens."

"You didn't choose your father's death."

"His life was his. I choose how to react. How to live life from there."

"You chose to be here?"

"I came. It doesn't mean that I like it. But now that I'm here, I decide how I respond and that conditions my situation.

My future is being made. And you: you came here. Nobody made you. You can't deny that."

"There was a deep pit lying in my path and I walked straight into it. I fell from one level of the maze to another, from the unreal to the surreal."

"Maybe that's what your real you chose for you. It gave you something to accomplish."

"But what is ever accomplished? I ascribe myself a task, like cleaning my bike, say. As I walk over to it with my cloth, I think I am carrying out that process, with a beginning, a middle and an end, but all I'm really doing is walking. When I get there, I move my hands in conformance with the mental image, I move this way and that, applying pressure and rubbing, and at some point I say that the thing is done. But that thing is an invented notion of mine. While there was movement, there was movement and that's all it was. Then it's gone, it's the past, it doesn't exist."

"But the bike is clean."

"Only as a comparison in my mind. Dirty and clean are subjective epithets that I ascribe to suit my own invented narrative. It is only clean, or black-and-white, to me. The bike doesn't know. It doesn't compare. It has no reality but the present."

"So why do anything?"

"With the way things are going, there won't be anything left to do. I will end up with an intelligent bike that knows just how clumsy my human hands are and will order and arrange its own robotic cleaning. Automation is a melting glacier sweeping us in its path and speeding up. People can deny it now but they won't be able to for much longer. We can escape here, but we can't escape our own irrelevance."

"Isn't irrelevance another of your invented notions?"

Yannick was silent.

"She's got you there, Homeless." Sven loomed before them. "It's time for beddy-byes."

"OK, goodnight," Anja said. "We're fine here." She took hold of Yannick's arm. This could be their chance. Wait for them to retire and we go!

"Not for me: for you. These two people will take you there."

"Take us where?" said Anja.

"Somewhere snug to spend the night."

There was nothing to be gained by resistance. Anja and Yannick allowed themselves to be guided by Breathless and the Witch out of the cavern and down one of tunnels.

"This is it," hissed the man that Anja still saw as a beast. "We're here. You need to get down on your knees to go inside." He held Yannick's wrist with surprising strength and placed his hand on a round opening in the wall at ground level. "The Soft Cave is all yours tonight. We'll come and get you in the morning."

Yannick crawled in and the Witch made sure that Anja followed, feeling like Gretel following a dumb Hansel into her larder. Two potties were pushed through the hole in the wall and Breathless indicated that he would take first watch outside.

• • • •

It was much warmer and distinctly airless in the new cave, whose floor was not just covered but tightly packed with cushions. These would be more than comfortable to recline on but proved difficult to climb over. They persevered, feeling like stubborn toddlers, exploring the limits of their cell. It was much bigger than either of them expected, probably enough for at least half the underground community to sleep in, and approximately round with a low, curved ceiling of hacked-out rock. The only way in or out was the narrow opening through which they had crawled.

The presence of the cushions was creepily incongruous, giving the clammy cellar the air of a squatted crypt, or a comfortable tomb. Of all shapes and sizes, fillings and textures, they were crammed in from wall to wall, and a variety of blankets and coverlets lay scattered around on top of them.

"How long do you think they'll keep us here?" said Anja. How long will the night be, she had wanted to ask.

"They have to let us out eventually," said Yannick, suppressing a rising attack of panic that only a forest clearing would relieve, to be beaten up under a high sky and thrown in a lake.

There was nothing more to be said, nothing to be done. They had been reminded of their true status with humiliating ease. They were prisoners who imagined that they might be free: to make the attempt to flee. That script had been tossed away. Their chance, if such it had been, was gone and all their earlier talk seemed foolish and vain. They were again, or still, artless, clueless and incapacitated in this dark and alien confinement, this horror without issue or end in sight.

Unable to reach across the futile comfort of their surroundings, they moved wordlessly apart, their cramped bodies and minds nestling into what solitary relief they could find. Distanced from all that they knew, distanced from each other, in barren silence.

. . . .

Yannick woke up sweating and dreaming. It was convoluted, improbable and unpleasant. There was no starlight shimmering on the ocean this time; he might instead be in its dense depth, scuppered in its darkest trench from where hope was banished and it was forgotten who he might even be. To his consternation, on feeling around with his hands, recognizing the cushions on which he lay and had slept, breathing in the thin, overheated air, he realized that the dream was true, or knew that it must be, that it was no dream. It was still happening and he was in it. His dreaming clogged the surface of his mind like black foam, a drifting froth that he needed to blow away.

"Are you there? Are you awake?"

"Yes," Anja said.

That element in the dream was true, also, then.

"Is there anyone else in here? Anyone?" he said louder.

There was no answer, no sound.

"It's too hot," he said.

Anja, who had been wide awake for some time, said nothing more. She had almost forgotten that he was there and his stirring and addressing her was unsettling, since he was close, much closer than she imagined, and except for a pair of knickers she was naked.

During the three or five or ten hours of her companion's sleeping, time now being immeasurable, she had gone on a voyage to nowhere and back. After floundering over the cushions to a space where she could have some privacy, she had sat back against an oversized pillow, hugged her knees to her chest and sworn quietly at the darkness. The escape unmade, helpless still within the prison walls and now in solitary, Anja hadn't wanted to know anything, hadn't wanted to think, and willed her mind a total blank. All she wanted to do was block it all out.

Like her attempt at home at meditative peace, it didn't last long. The compulsive desire to engineer a successful outcome would not leave her in peace. What couldn't be resolved in the cavern wouldn't be resolved within the tighter constraint of the Soft Cave, but that didn't stop her mind from playing out the scenarios. Each one tormented her in the sunken oubliette, where the shipwreck of their plot floated in her mind. When she sought to calm herself, the intention morphed into a painful desire to take out all the cushions, sweep and mop the cave, all of it, floor, walls and roof, and leave it impeccable. In the end, tears rolled down her cheeks and she sobbed. She cried until she had cried herself out and nothing more was left but a sense of shame. Not even her father's death had defeated her like this, so thoroughly.

She had then drifted in the doldrums, in and out of sleep, until waking with a start. It seemed later, much later. Whether it was night, or day, or evening, she could not know, but she had the sensation of having missed something. She had a fierce desire for it to be six am and a run to be awaiting her through the freezing wind of the streets. Instead, it was hot and clammy and there was nowhere to go. The moist air trapped beneath the cave's low ceiling was like steam in her face and her lungs sought for a little more oxygen than it could provide. Anja felt enormous in the amorphous space, like a balloon inflated to fill the entire troglodyte dome, pressing her membrane against its rocky surface as if exploring and feeling out its every crevice.

Anja had slept in her clothes and her elemental enormity was sweltering. In the sauna-like atmosphere, she now shed the long coat, boots and socks. Her pullovers were history, but she still wore two tops and a bra that were as much of a burden as her thick cotton trousers. She pulled them all off and tied one garment to another in a linked sequence, a supple prisoner's chain that she could drag with her and claim whenever she needed to. After which, the world was her boudoir and the hooded darkness bore a hole that she could breathe through: breathe and pass through, like a smoky spirit. There was no body and she was weightless, existing only as every atom in the cave, like a power, a goddess. Because there was nothing, she could have been anything, but she chose the nothing, the numb awareness.

When Yannick spoke, she had replied involuntarily before holding still. What was he doing so close to her? Had he slithered over to her like some man-snake? She dared not move in case the cushions that were supporting her slipped or gave in the wrong way and she toppled into him. At the same time, she was dreadfully aware that she had not showered for at least two days and horrified that he might smell her. She held her upper arms tight to her sides to prevent the escape of underarm odour, kept her hands on her breasts and wondered how she might retrieve a top, at least, and put it on.

"Do you know what day it is?" he asked.

"It might be the twenty-third still. But it could be Christmas Eve already," her voice croaked. She needed some water.

"We have to be strong and get through this," he proffered, for want of anything better to say.

Yannick's commonplace conversation encouraged her. She really did remain unseen. She would continue as if picking up on their earlier conversation.

"Get to the surface, like your submarine. Only it's not a movie," she said. "We can't just sit and wait and hope for a happy ending."

"But we can't do anything, either."

"Can't we? Can't you?"

"There's someone on guard all the time." She sounded riled, thought Yannick. "I can only find one boot," he said.

"You should have tied their laces together."

"What do you think's going to happen?"

"In the next five minutes? Days? To us? To our world?"

"To us."

"What would you like to happen?" She wished she had worded that differently. "If you visualize a positive outcome, it potentiates that."

"Anything would beat this. But it's just as bad or worse up there. In the world."

"Why be so... so miserable?"

"What's there not to be miserable about?"

"Do you think they're going to kill us, is that it?"

"They don't have to. We're already buried."

"Don't be so defeatist! Goddamn!"

"Don't shout in my ear."

As she had feared, a cushion had shifted under her backside, leaning her towards him at the most awkward of angles. She felt like a human tower of Pisa to which the wrong adjustment could prove fatal. To use a hand to push down and pivot away would mean exposing an armpit as well as the breast that it was clutching—not that he would see her nipple, but all the same...

"Are you angry with me?" he said.

If she replied at this proximity, he would think she was murmuring in his ear. On the other hand, she couldn't not say anything.

"Why should I be?" she said gently.

"For getting you into this fix."

"We are all responsible for our own actions. I got myself into this."

"Whatever *this* is," he said.

She could sense his face and attention turned towards her own.

"It's alright," she said.

"Isn't it strange?"

"Which bit of strange in the strangeness do you mean?"

"How everything is so basic in the dark. Primitive. Like it comes down to touching. It all starts from touch and feeling. Movement, obstruction, pressure. Hot and cold. The other senses are a refinement of touch. Tasting and smelling, analysing like human chemistry sets. Sensing vibrations in the ears, light waves in the eyes, even."

"Tell me about normal life," she said. "Before this. About yours."

"Nothing to tell. I don't believe in boring people with it," he turned his face away.

"Alright, if you don't want to." Anja knew how cross that sounded. Her cheeks were flushed and her skin from the neck down felt the same. It was getting muggier in their drowsy hollow and the strain was just too much: she couldn't maintain the posture any longer. The plump cushion slipped out from beneath her and she collapsed onto one side, where her head lay jammed between the cushion that Yannick sat on and a beanbag. She might have given up there and then but his feet stank. Still protecting her breasts with her hands, she took a quick breath, jacked herself up, rolled over and wriggled away using just her legs, until she felt that she could let go and right herself, sitting on something firmer. She grabbed hold of her clothing train and sat up straight, pretending that nothing had happened. Her heart told her otherwise.

"Tell me about you," he said.

"Alright," she cleared her throat. "I go the gym twice a week. Or I used to."

Had he not noticed anything?

"Why do you go?" he asked.

"What?"

"Why do you go to the gym?"

"What kind of question is that? Don't you want to be a healthy person? Don't you want to push... What do you want, anyway? Don't you want anything?"

"Every time I want something and move towards it, it disappears around a corner. Or the corner itself disappears and maybe there's the thing I want but it's a hologram, ungraspable, because there's no context for it to be real in."

"You mustn't give up."

"I do want to get us out of here, Anja."

"Good."

"Kiss and make up! Kiss and make up!"

The little girl whose name was Abegael had sneaked silently into the cave, right up to them, and she was now jumping up and down on the cushions. Accidentally on purpose, she fell into Anja.

"She's not wearing any clothes! She's nuddy nuddy!"

Anja crawled desperately away, as fast as she could manage, dragging her clothing with her. Not until she found the wall did she stop and start dressing, beginning with her bra.

"What's your name?" said Yannick, although he remembered perfectly well.

"Abegael," she said proudly.

"My name's Yannick"

"No, it's not, it's Pisshead, hee-hee, roly-poly Pisshead!"

"Do you live down here all the time?"

"No, silly, I live in my house with my mummies."

"Do you know the way there?"

"No. But I can go to the park and I can go to the sweets shop."

"Could you take us there?"

"You have to go with a grown-up."

"We're grown-ups."

"A proper grown-up. You're sighted. Mummy said so."

"I see," said Yannick.

"Which seems to disqualify you," said Anja, who had rejoined them.

"You could get lost like our dog. Do you have a puppy or a cat or a hamster? I would like a dog and a hamster that doesn't bite because it hurts."

"Abby?"

"Mummy, mummy, here, mummy! I'm with Pisshead and his girlfriend."

"Don't call him that, Abegael. His name's Yannick. It's a nice name. And she's Anja. Hallo, you two, I brought you some pancakes. Careful, there's lingonberries and spiced crème fraiche on top of them."

The woman Anja thought of as Almost Normal slid across the cushions and handed them a tray with plates and a fork each. There was the unmistakable pungency of hot coffee to go with it, which somehow amplified the smell of Yannick's socks.

"I can't," Anja said. "I just can't. I need to see it."

"That's not possible, I'm sorry," said the woman. "We have none of your light."

"I thought most blind people could see even a little bit."

"You mean the partials. We are the true blind. Why don't you get that? You people never stop talking about seeing, but to us it means nothing."

"It might be crawling with ants," Anja said.

"I'll try it for you," Yannick offered. "If it's not alright, I'll tell you."

"Alright."

Anja waited.

"It's good. Give me your hand."

Anja guided his hand with a forkful of pancake to her mouth. God, she was hungry as well as thirsty.

"It's not allowed to eat in the Soft Cave," Abegael objected.

"That's quite right, Abby. But today..."

"It's Christmas," guessed Anja, tasting the berries and gulping some coffee. "It's morning time, I assume."

"Christmas! Christmas! Can we go home?"

"Yes, can we go home?"

"Mummy, please?"

"That depends on the festive goodwill of the mayor."

"Shit!" said Yannick.

"Language!" Anja admonished her companion in front of the child.

"I spilt coffee on my leg."

"Eat properly. You have to keep it all on your plate," Abegael told him.

"Sven's on his way to the Town Hall right now," said her mother.

"She wasn't wearing any clothes, but she is now."

"What if the mayor says no?" asked Anja.

There was no reply. Anja wondered what was going through the woman's head.

"If you were my mummy, would you give me Lego for Christmas?" asked Abegael.

"Not if you were a telltale," said Anja.

"Nuddy! Nuddy and Pisshead!"

"Abby!"

"Listen, I need... women's things: you know," said Anja. "I have them in my backpack."

"Oh, right, of course. Well, I'll check with whoever's on duty, but I think it's alright for you to come out now. We're just waiting for Sven. Everyone's getting ready."

When permission came through, they exited impatiently, getting to their feet in the tunnel, where the comparatively fresher subterranean air perked them up almost immediately. They placed their pisspots on the ground with a couple of others waiting to be collected and the woman took their breakfast trays off them. She led them back to the cavern and round to their bench. It felt like having privileges restored. Or being given a second chance.

"Do you need the bathroom?" she asked Anja.

"No, it's alright. But a bottle of water, please."

When they sat down, they could visualize precisely where they were and where they needed to go.

The table and chairs were being set up in the Middle and people were taking their places, talking and listening, making preparations for Sven's return and news that might go either way. It represented an unwanted obstacle in their way, but they could go round it, Yannick whispered to her.

Anja started to put on her parka, then changed her mind. Its rustling was simply too loud and would give them away. She had forgotten to ask Almost Normal about the missing mittens, but in an inside pocket of the parka she found her thermal hat. She would settle for that and the soft felt coat over her long-sleeved tops.

Abegael arrived with two small plastic bottles of drinking water.

"Abegael: thanks for the games of dominoes," said Yannick.

"You're a good girl, really," said Anja.

"It's alright," said the girl. "I won't tell."

She left them wondering what that meant. Wondering, also, when a good opportunity might arise and how would they recognize it if it did? There was nobody else on their bench, no one there to notice if they got up and walked away. Yannick felt Anja tap his arm nine times.

It meant Now.

• • • •

Three short taps, three longer ones, three short ones was their agreed sign for an escape. The universal SOS in Morse code. Yannick took her hand and stood up.

They walked to the nearest rope and let it guide them to the Middle, making way for three people coming the other way and halting at the end stanchion, whose cap had four raised dots. At the table, just a few steps away, familiar voices could be heard. Anya and Yannick might have had quite different images of the Wolf, the Witch, Old Father, Almost Normal and Breathless Beast sitting there, but a projected three-dimensional image of the necessity of passing them by unnoticed was something they shared virtually identically. Anja pulled left and Yannick followed her lead. They found the next post (four dots also) and kept going around the table, past Old Father and behind Almost Normal's back, until Anja's hand touched another metal upright and she squeezed Yannick's hand . She read the top with her fingertips. Two bumps. She put Yannick's hand on it to tell him. It was theirs. They followed its rope to the matching stanchion at the other end, where their hands slid down to its base. The wool was still there, wound round and tied in a knot. They stayed down at ground level and moved off, letting the loose fibre run through a hand, entering the tunnel almost immediately and leaving the light hubbub of the bunker behind.

Anja's Fair Isle sweater took them past one passageway branching off left and turned them down the next. They felt confident enough to lift the wool off the ground and go forward with greater ease. When the tension slackened, they were obliged to slow and feel a way hand over hand, but then it would tense up again. They were getting the hang of it. After two more turns, right and left, Anja felt the knot where she had tied on the yellow sweater. There was now, she remembered, a longish, straight stretch of tunnel before the next turn right, and they might almost have taken it at a jog had it not been for the sound of someone approaching. *Cluk-cluk-cluk* went the slow, regular tongue of a blind person staying clear of the walls, adjusting to the mini-echoes. Anja and Yannick dropped the wool and stopped. There was barely room for two people to pass by each other in the narrow tunnel and even if they could hide against the wall, their soft bodies would annul those sonar *cluks* and they would be found out equally. It was too late in any case: the walker was upon them already. Yannick pulled Anja into him to make a single obstruction on the left and cleared his throat to announce their presence.

The footsteps stopped. Someone stood right in front of them, silently, but only a few seconds. "Move over," said an elderly voice crossly. "Keep to the right!" They obeyed, flattening themselves against the right-hand side of the tunnel, while the old man went past them. "Idiots," they heard him mumble, before resuming his grandfather clock rhythm onwards. The Bat, Anja decided. Furry-headed, moving along with curled talons and hunched, coal-black wings.

The two escapees felt around for the line of wool on the ground and soon resumed their progress, letting hope light the way through the monotonous, tortuous underworld. They pulled themselves gently forward, careful that their wispy guideline should not break and leave them stranded, turning here, turning there, shoulders scraping the rock wall, hauling themselves cautiously along. They were getting there. Their submarine was rising. When suddenly they reached the end of the line, a four-handed search quickly discovered that the wall was already open. The punctilious old man hadn't closed it back up after his toilet visit. The levered-out stone blocks lay piled on the ground together with a long crowbar, which Yannick took. They clambered through the hole and into the broad sewer.

They had already talked about which way to go. If they went left, it would be in the face of every warning they had been given about something that lay down that way, something that people wouldn't even talk about. The thing that shrieked. To the right, as far as they knew, once they got past the rudimentary WC, the sewer lay quietly open and pointed like the empty finger of a glove to a freedom still contained, but explorable.

They felt their way along the wall, treading cautiously once more over the curved flooring of the town drain. It was blessedly quiet. Tired as they were and full of dread, neither of them had felt so alive. Keen to use the facility, they made way and waited for each other when they came to the WC. Then moved on, as quickly as they dared while staying close and in contact, keeping pace with their unspoken or whispered thoughts—don't stop, we're doing great, we're getting out, just keep moving—their right hands held high to trail the brickwork, hoping against hope to hit the rung of a ladder that rose to their true world, for a piece of iron pain that would light up an exit sign.

For a long time, both of them growing tired as the buoyancy of adrenaline wore off, feeling underfed and doubtful, they came across nothing. When they did, it was not anything they could possibly have expected.

Anya, who was leading, stopped and held back a hand to halt Yannick. She had heard a heavy thud of shoes. Someone had stamped, or landed on their feet, about ten paces away. There was a rattling noise and distant shouting. Now the someone was busy with something. They waited. It was likely that they had gone unnoticed. A scratching sound produced a visible blur in the perpetual void, a blue lamp that they drew instinctively back from, and then flashing silver burst out into the air, burning jagged gashes into the tender cells of their dormant retinas, upon which the firework exploded—and all hell let loose. Bangers and crackling jumping jacks turned the local environment into a battle zone of blinding flashes and rapid blasts and machine gun ratatatat. Ruby red stars were pumped into their vicinity to self-detonate with pressurized booms and splinter into slow-burning magnesium that hung in the air; rockets flew wildly, clattering straight into the wall or zooming down the tunnel to rupture like death stars and send back echoing thunderclaps that jarred their hearing.

Anya and Yannick hunkered down, shielding their eyes from the blitz, torn between fleeing back the way they had come and freezing like rabbits as they suffered the crazy electric pain of the light and the violent explosions.

At the nuclear centre of it all capered the incendiary kobold himself. Exposed to the full force of his own effulgence, flares burning and fizzing about his feet and grinning like an inebriated Lucifer, Sven flung his firebrands every which way, blocking any advance with an exaggerated display of pandemonium and menace. He took one last item from a cardboard box, a fat cylindrical firework, touched its blue touch paper with his smoldering lighter stick, and threw it the other way down the tunnel, blocking his ears with his fingers. It exploded with a salvo shaking Yannick and Anja to the core and whooshing them with a paroxysm of torched, expelled air from the sewer's gaseous interior.

As the last scintillations and flames died down, Sven picked up a slim briefcase and a stick and stepped towards them like nothing more than a businessman on his way home, albeit one delivered of a flaming fit of lunacy. The young people got unsteadily to their feet. Yannick still had the crowbar, but he just wasn't going to use it on the man, no matter how treacherous his machinations or their predicament.

"Quickly," Anja said.

"Come back," they heard him say, as they started retreating, pulling each other along and breaking into a trot, Yannick stumbling and falling, grazing his hands but getting straight back up again, struggling to catch up with Anja as she ran with fierce intent and monosyllabic footfalls, no-no, no-no, back down the tunnel of hope.

• • • •

Little more than an hour earlier, Sven had caused similar consternation in a roomful of the most powerful people in the country.

While they waited with scant conviction in the Mayoral Chamber for the supposed reappearance of a blind man, the Prime Minister, who was now directing operations herself, and the head of Homeland Security had been trying and failing to put into effect a successful operation that would reconnect the capital with its power supply. Rapidly. Before its descent into chaos was irreversible.

Standing at the window, in what he considered unjustified disgrace and executively excluded from proceedings, was the mayor. Gazing out over the grand square like this had often helped him think when faced with dilemmas and, in any case, it was preferable to looking around his militarily commandeered office. All the working electronic equipment in the city seemed to be concentrated in this long room of shiny wood and thick carpeting. Supervised by an unsmiling senior aide, personnel monitored screens and listened in to wavelengths, while the PM and her small team occupied the mayor's polished cedar table.

Once the prime suspect had slipped through his fingers the day before, robbing him of the chance to take the credit for a crucial breakthrough, the mayor had had no choice but to let national government know about it. He had quickly passed from chief authority to little more than chastened bystander in his own Town Hall, but it still looked as though he mattered, which is what usually counted in local politics, and he still had his opinions and a voice. It might be a national emergency, but it was his city and he knew it better than the politicos.

Even though he couldn't make out much from this range, the mayor's eyes were fixed on the distant security post that was now the sole access point to the irregularly lit square. The guards were on high alert for any approaching citizen and a radio would report any eventuality to this their operations room, but something made him keep staring. When a flash and a thud rocked a not-so-distant street—one of increasingly frequent small explosions and fires studding the benighted carapace of the city—his attention was diverted briefly to the site and expression of discontent, before returning to scan the square again and focus on its checkpoint. The wise minds in the chamber had considerable might and intelligence at their disposal, but in this rare storm their technological statecraft was stranded. He fixed an unreasonable hope on something as simple as a man with a donkey, or a blind beggar, passing into the frozen square to save them all.

They had spent the early hours establishing what they knew.

The outage had nothing to do with the nuclear facility or its substations. The electrical supply and tension were in good order. The power was there, but it was just not getting through. "There is no power cut," the chief engineer had confirmed. "But the power is cut."

"I want answers, not riddles," the Prime Minister snapped at him.

Her country was losing its nerve, too. Centuries of peaceful cohabitation and prosperous development had inculcated a universally respected civic concord that was the envy of the world. It was the single quality that their culture held dearer than any other, but when the country's leader looked out from the top floor of the capital's Town Hall, she, too, could see glimmers of fires that were burning from accident, design or desperation. Access to food, water and heating had become critical in the space of a few hours. They were now well into a third day. It was 8:25 a.m. on Christmas Eve and reports of violent assault, looting and vandalism were no longer isolated incidents. Neighbour was turning against neighbour. Deaths were being registered and people were starting to panic as their nominally Christian leaders failed them and a god named Chaos filled the psychic vacuum. The international press was already suggesting that the Nordic capital so proud of its medieval heritage was declining into crude, medieval conditions. Their whole way of life had been undermined with such terrible ease and the technical engineers had yet to devise or explain a solution.

"The only way to achieve outages like this, by entire sectors or groups of sectors," said the reprimanded engineer, "is to physically cut through the power lines: to sever them at multiple sites. Until we know the exact locations of these sites, we're working in the dark. We'd have to dig up half the city to find them and fix them."

"Which would take?"

"Weeks, maybe months, Prime Minister."

"Could it be a malicious hack?" asked the director of Homeland Security.

The engineer shook his head. "No, it doesn't work like that. Hostile communications technology could conceivably cause mischief at source, in the nuclear station's network. It can't interrupt the flow of energy. My engineering team is pretty confident it's like I said. The diagnostics programme points to physically compromised lines."

"So if you were a terrorist, what would you use to do this and how would you do it?"

"You need a piece of equipment that fires a bolt to cut the mains cable. It's a very hazardous procedure. The obvious and usually the only way would be to dig down from the street consulting a network plan and use a device to locate the live cable. But we haven't found any illicit digs that might take us to the breakage points. I think we've ruled that out?"

"That's correct," one of the Prime Minister's aides confirmed.

"They're in the sewers," the mayor spoke up. "They're right underneath us. They've hacked through from there."

"With all due respect, Mr Mayor," said the engineer, "that's impossible. We know exactly where the power lines run through the city. It's all mapped out. The major sections you'd have to hit to cause outages like this are quite a distance from the sewers."

"What kind of capability are we talking about here?" The Homeland Security director, whose name was Zoltan, was looking at a screen where the engineer's network was showing. The complexity of it was startling.

"Well, if you don't dig down from the street, then somehow you have to be down there already. Like some superhuman mole."

"There are foreign powers, one in particular springs immediately to mind, who would want to see what damage they can do," said the Director. "But this aggression is so crude, so hands-on, that it just doesn't make sense. Which brings us to your visitor," he turned to the city's mayor. "And the absurd note he left. Can he really be our man? If it is him, why come here and effectively offer himself up? How could such an amateur be behind the gravest attack this country has suffered since the Second World War? And why pretend to be a blind man? We're nowhere near solving this."

"He said he'd be back today. I believe him," said the mayor.

"If he does, he's all yours, Zoltan," said the Prime Minister. "I do think it's him. The timings and sector numbers on his note tally precisely with the five outages. And there is only one possible way in which the strange demands can make sense: he really is blind. And apparently not just out for himself but for his entire collective. So we might expect him to have help and support from amongst them. How many blind people do we have? In this city?" she asked the team of aides hovering on the edge of the conversation.

"On average, 0.34% of a population is totally blind. That would make five hundred and thirty citizens," came the answer. "Triple that if you include the almost or virtually blind."

"Which would make for quite an organization if they all plotted against their government," said the PM. "How many would be essential to carry out the sabotage as you see it?" she asked the chief engineer.

"Five. A person has to be there to operate the cable spiker and there were five separate, physically distanced events which between them cut off all eight sectors of the city. The incidents happened within a few minutes of each other, so it was clearly a coordinated action involving five individuals as a bare minimum."

"Information on disaffected blind people, online threats tagged with blind or disabled, robbery or purchase of any devices that can cut power lines, locations where the cuts could or must have taken place," ordered Zoltan of his people.

"We're running out of time," the mayor spoke the unspoken thought of them all.

"If your man does show up, we are at least prepared," said the Prime Minister. "We go along with him. We give him his contract in Braille, which is a legally binding language, and let him think he's got the better of us. We give him whatever he asks for, whatever it will take for him to lead us to the faults and restore power. Then we nail him. He deserves it."

A movement in the plaza's chiaroscuro caught the mayor's eye and he looked down. A burly shadow was coming straight towards them. As it came within range of the floodlights set up on the roof of the Town Hall, the shadow became a man in a heavy overcoat bent against the bitter cold, who now stopped, listening to his surroundings.

"That's him!" shouted the mayor. "It's him!"

Zoltan ran to join him at the window and seconds later the room was in uproar.

• • • •

Sven could smell burning and hear distant tumult. Not far behind him, a chant of protest rang out like an alarm and something was being drummed, maybe a car roof. From closer by came another kind of shout and a rush of bodies and his arms were seized. He hadn't expected to be lifted and carried through the same Public Entrance that he had used the previous day, but it saved him the trouble of finding his way and got him that much more quickly out of the cold. One got used to the native warmth of the underground tunnels and coming up top was enough to stupefy a person.

Ignoring the barked questions, smiling behind his dark glasses, he submitted a brusque search before being declared physically inoffensive.

"I've come to see the Mayor," he said.

"Hold his head still."

"Let me through," Sven said gruffly, while a pencil light was shone into his eyes.

"The prisoner will be quiet," the guard duty officer informed him and unmuted the radio mike. "No sir, no ID, nothing. Caucasian, fair hair, about 65 years, 1.70, 85 kilos. Apparently so: yes, sir. The subject's eyes do not dilate. Yes, sir. Take him in," he ordered the squad leader standing by. "As Prime Object."

· · · ·

They would be making their way up the stairs even now. The lift programming was too unreliable on back-up power and even the PM had had to use the back stairs.

"It's him, that's an affirmative," the mayor heard the confirmation over the intercom loud speaker. A positive ID had just been made by one of the staff who had seen Sven go in and out yesterday.

"A traditional burgher who insists on talking to his mayor," the Prime Minister told him. "Act as if you're in charge."

· · · ·

The room smelled of wood polish and old money, thought Sven, when they brought him in.

"Sit him down."

From his side of the table, the mayor studied the grubby man, who might have been one of the undesirables they had had cleared from the public square. He leaned forward.

"I'm the Mayor. Tell me what I need to know."

"You need to know that your citizens are not a nuisance or a demand on resources. We are the whole point of having resources. You are public servants," said the tramp-like figure to the room. "And we are the public. Who else is here?"

Had he been able to see, the blind man would have been looking round at the country's elected Prime Minister, three of her cabinet ministers, her spin doctor, personal private assistants, video equipment recording the encounter, heavily armed police and military agents, coloured lights blinking on a series of devices loaded into wall sockets and a very bright spotlight directed onto his face. Sven could sense their presence, feel the heat, smell the guns, but his opaque eyes registered nothing.

"A higher authority than me," said the mayor.

"I thought we might have company," said Sven. "Do we have legal agreement of our demands?"

The mayor pushed the Braille document under his fingers and Sven immediately went about reading it at speed.

"The seal at the foot of each page bears the stamp of the Government Office. You can have it checked by a lawyer if you wish."

"It's all there," Sven said. It was, even if hedged in all around by legalese. He had been pleased to note that the subsidized meals service had been included and restored. It meant five days a week that he didn't have to cook and he was especially partial to the fish chowder option on Fridays.

"Before you leave here with that, you help us restore full power throughout the city. First, you have some explaining to do. Who are you? What is your organization and who are its members?"

"I'm no one," said Sven. "We are the people in this society who you overlook. But not anymore. Not today, anyway. I will take you to the five cut-off points. You'll need to bring your engineers to fix the damage. Let's go," he stood up.

"Start by telling us who you are," said another man's voice.

"Oh, that's alright, I don't mind waiting." Sven sat down again. "I've got no plans for Christmas."

The Prime Minister said something in Zoltan's ear. I can make him tell us, he informed her. She shook her head. She wasn't going to delay. They would decide what to do with him afterwards. Even through the reinforced windows, the angry voices of the protestors could be heard across the square.

"Let him take you to the sabotaged points and get them fixed. Go now. Just don't lose him," she said to an unconvinced Zoltan, who still hadn't recovered his composure since their prime suspect had somehow ghosted through the impenetrable security of his checkpoint, which had been silent and ignorant throughout.

The PM motioned over her spin doctor. "Homeland Security will take charge of this phase," she told him. "What do we tell the media? How do we play it?"

"Unidentified terrorists," said the young man. "That's what Homeland have them down as anyway. It's either that or you admit that the country and its government were brought to its knees by a blind old man."

"That's it, then," decided the Prime Minister. "This affair is now a state secret in the interests of national security. There's no need for anyone to know."

There was a short wait while a stick was sent for, one of the new intelligent instruments that were itemized in the blind people's charter and that Sven insisted on taking with him. Then the old man then led them off, carrying both his new stick and a light briefcase with the government order conceding all points in the list of demands. Accompanying and guarding the sturdy but slow senior citizen, a formidable train of soldiers, electrical engineers, a communications team and motley other agents moved across the icy flagstones of the square in strange convoy, two spotlights from the Town Hall roof lighting the way and another from a helicopter hovering directly overhead.

Sven was guided past the kiosk from which he had emerged unseen not long before and then out through the checkpoint. Riot police pushed back the protestors, many of whom fell silent at the sight of the ill-kempt, infirm figure leading out such a formidable task force. Their curiosity aroused, they left their station and joined the end of the procession instead, following on behind with their flaming torches casting long, flickering shadows, as the blind man headed them all down a long avenue, striking his long, luminescent stick into the ground like a wizard's staff. A stately, eccentric expedition bent on seeking the source of darkness.

"There is a Burger King thirty metres ahead on the left," said the stick. "Currently closed."

Sven chose his steps in the careful manner of a blind pedestrian, a slow pace that irritated his military escort at the same time that it slackened their concentration.

"How far are we going, mate?" the force leader asked Sven.

"Another six blocks," he lied.

"Street crossing. Traffic lights. No signal. Stay alert," said the stick as they crept across a junction.

"Do you know where you are?" asked the force leader.

"I think so," said Sven.

The leader sighed and radioed in the status of their tedious progress.

A little further on, temporary roadworks shielded by signs and corrugated iron panels obliged them to pass through a narrow gap. Two machine-gun carrying soldiers with infrared goggles pushed through first to lead the way, followed in single file by Sven and his throng of followers, held up behind him in the bottleneck. Sven felt his way through, nervously tapping the iron panel on the right until it came to an end and then performed an act for which he had prepared himself a hundred times, using the trapdoors in the kiosks for practice.

His stick located the manhole on the right whose cover had been pushed carefully off and to one side earlier by the invisible hands of the Wolf. He tossed stick and briefcase down the invisible opening in the darkness and before the agent directly behind him could react, jumped into the round hole himself, pulling closed the heavy cover by means of a solid chain welded into its base. He swore, having bashed and bruised his hip with a clumsy entry, but held onto the ladder and hooked the carabiner on the other end of the chain to a rung, so that the manhole cover was secured and could not be lifted off.

He climbed down the ladder and dropped the last two feet to the ground, grimacing as his arthritic knees and skinned hip took his weight. Shouting and a fierce clonking of the manhole cover above his head caused him to cringe and hesitate, but the rattling chain held.

• • • •

In the sewer, Sven felt around for the briefcase and stick and gathered them to him, then located what he thought of as his nuclear deterrent, a large cardboard box containing a cornucopia of festive fireworks and a biscuit tin with lighters. He grabbed the fireworks and started setting them off indiscriminately, throwing them from him at the first fizz and holding rockets by the tip of their long sticks. The more he lit, the more they boomed and burst and crackled, the barrage amplified and rebounded by the tunnel's sound box, the more a mad levity overtook the man. He revelled in the deafening cacophony, throwing bangers by the handful, not caring when a mega-rocket scorched his wrist before screeching off down the tunnel. When he got to the end of the box and his hands came upon the household artillery's pièce de résistance, he lifted it out and considered it. Its bulk and weight warned of a considerable payload of gunpowder. He concentrated, ignited it and threw it up the sewer as far as he could, crouching and sticking stubby fingers in his ear holes. The stunning detonation that seconds later rocked the tunnel blew his hair up wildly and took his breath away. It took several seconds for him to become aware of another person standing there not far away. Two people, in fact. Who had just been hit by the same flabbergasting sound and heat wave as himself. Were they alright? Nobody was supposed to be in here. It wasn't safe. His people knew to stay at the base and wait for him there. Picking up the briefcase and stick, he moved towards them, but they had already turned and were moving away.

"Quickly," said the girl.

"Come back," said Sven.

It was the bloody sightseers.

If they were running wild, this could get very sticky. They had no idea of anything.

. . . .

A considerable distance away through the many-branching tunnels, the rock floor of the underground bunker had trembled and everyone gathered there together knew that this was it.

. . . .

On the freezing city street, the force leader had communicated the situation to the Town Hall HQ and received an answer. Given the evidence of fighting capability directly beneath where they stood, the directive was to not force entry there. Instead, he should send two teams to enter through the proximate manholes fore and aft and converge from both sides on the target, who would be trapped. The order was a capture, whenever possible, but all necessary force could be employed.

. . . .

They moved as fast they could safely go without slipping down the concave floor into the sewer's sludge, skirting the wall all the way, coming to the breach that crossed over to the tunnel complex, which would only take them back into the absurd dungeon, and pressing on past the other way: the way they had been warned not to go. Perhaps because it in fact provided an easy egress, Anja reasoned with herself and Yannick. It was all a blind man's bluff and they would all of a sudden find themselves out of there. Yannick had no mind to disagree. Somewhat unsure on his feet at the best of times, he concentrated on trying to keep up with the small, purposeful girl who had already broken into a jog and was speeding up.

After a hundred metres or so, he noted a change in the sewer's agricultural odour. If there really was danger here, some lurking Minotaur, it had rotten-meaty breath. The trickle of effluent down the centre of the voluminous brick pipe had also built up, mounting the curved side, so that watery sewage was fouling his shoes and making progress so slithery and slimy that he was about to call out to Anja, who was skipping along ahead, when her footfalls fell silent and a dull grunt issued from her. She had stopped dead.

"Anya?" called Yannick.

There was no reply.

"Anya!"

He advanced, grasping at the noxious air and plunged his right hand into a mass of goo, where it was squeezed and held tight. With the desperation of disgust but considerable difficulty, he tugged it free of the loathsome, insisting handshake.

Anja groaned right next to him.

He took hold of her, pulling her towards him, but she stayed put. She was stuck fast in the same gunk. Yannick still carried the long crowbar that was used to open up the sewer from the tunnels. He established an area of brick wall with a gluey hand and then struck it with the crowbar, using the sparks that flew up to catch the briefest glimpse of Anya's form. He struck again and again, chips of brick scattering to a high-pitched ring, and three spark flashes later became aware of the strange immensity of her adversary. A mythic creature would have been a godsend compared with the colossal fatberg which held her in its glutinous embrace.

She had run into its squishiness at speed and sunk straight in. Once it had her, it grabbed with its rubbery gloop and wouldn't let go. She had been able to turn half her face out of it, but her torso and limbs were stuck fast, immovable.

"Nnnnnnnh," she moaned.

Yannick took hold of her under the armpits and pulled for all he was worth. It was worse than useless. The fatberg seemed to treat it as a game and each time that Yannick pulled, it sucked her further in.

"Yaah," Anja tried to say his name.

Yannick stood horrified. He dared not use the heavy crowbar on it for fear of hitting the girl. He turned and howled his wretchedness to the tunnel.

At that, he heard muffled shouts, followed by a pause and then loud reports interspersed with heavy thuds in the fatberg, which wobbled. There were people on the other side of the gross mountain and they were shooting at it.

In Yannick's blackness, a white line appeared. It moved around his field of non-vision like a dancing neon strip light and then Sven emerged. He was wielding the luminous stick in his right hand like a lightsaber and approaching as quickly as he was able.

"Homeless?" called Sven.

"Yes," he replied. He was that and so much less.

"We have to get out," panted Sven. "They'll be coming."

"It's Anja. She's stuck in the goo."

"You have to get her out. We have to go now," insisted Sven.

"Hold your stick up. Give me light," Yannick said.

Sven held up his stick. He began to turn it in his fist like a swizzle stick and it gleamed a meager light onto the girl, who was being engulfed by slow, powerful suction into the yellowish putrescence. Above her head, her soft knitted hat glared like a red pustule as it disappeared. The toxic stink was intolerable.

Thwack, thwack, thump, thump went the bullets into the hideous mass of congealed grease, fat and sanitary products. It whistled a shrill complaint. Like a primitive form of life, the lardy excrescence had grown to clog the tunnel almost entirely, leaving only pipe holes at the top to screech and moan when the tide came in. It was so obese that for now, at least, it was stopping the bullets.

Using the sharp, forked end of the iron crowbar, Yannick dug and scraped at the slimy gunk that had already surrounded so much of the girl, and when that didn't work, started hacking at the blubber monster for real. Lumps of it came away and plopped to the ground or into the deep pool of blocked sewage below. He hewed and gouged and Anja's left arm became visible and he was able to pull it free. Careful not to puncture her flesh, he moved up and down either side of her body, wrenching out one fatty glob after another. When with a grunt Anja ripped her right elbow out of its trap, he was able to get his arms all the way round her and, with a parting, farty squelch, drag her slobberingly free.

Anja sat on the unwholesome ground, convulsing. "Ah, ah," was all she said between heaves, but there was no time, Sven was already leaving and the little light with him. Yannick looked quickly around for her things. Her woolly hat had been swallowed up but of her backpack there was no sign, either. It had tumbled off somewhere in the hopeless shadow, or into the sewer's pool to drown. Yannick lifted Anya to her feet and they hobbled together after the blind troublemaker.

They reached and passed through the gap in the wall, where Sven told Yannick to replace the blocks as best he could, and they hurried along the now welcome tunnels in what felt like a kind of safety.

• • • •

When it became clear that the blind man had gotten away again, giving the slip to Homeland Security and a multitudinous entourage, the mayor's smirk was irrepressible. He couldn't help it and he shouldn't—people were undoubtedly dying on his watch in the inhuman conditions— but he liked the man now. What's more, he had been proven right.

"I told you they were in the sewers," he said to Zoltan.

"Do be quiet," said the Prime Minister, who was listening closely in to the radioed progress reports.

The forward manhole team had been thwarted by the fatberg, unimpressed by their firepower, and were now laying explosive charges into its body jelly.

The aft manhole team had been unimpeded and were advancing even now from the opposite direction. The radio pinged. They team leader had something to report.

"A WC, bucket, water and soap. They've been using this place as a toilet."

The mayor guffawed.

"What are you waiting for? Get him!" ordered Zoltan.

• • • •

"We have it: they agreed to everything. Let's go!" said Sven to the assembled blind, ready and waiting in the bunker. He drank back half the breakfast coffee offered to him at the Middle table. "Make sure we've got everybody. You know who's in front of you and who's behind you," he called out. "Leave nothing behind that can be traced back to you, or it comes back on us all. A last act of solidarity. Merry fucking Christmas. Two columns, let's go."

There was a nervous and excited flurry of activity all around. Someone lost their bearings and walked into the table, knocking over a bottle of water. "Mind my coffee," chided Sven, even though he was already taking his place at the rear in his column, keeping the sightseers in front of him.

A sickly scent of patchouli announced the Witch. "Here," she said, "and here," pressing into Yannick and Anya's hands their mobile phone, as if they were passports to take them back across the frontier separating them from their world. The mobiles were all they got back. As the Witch moved off,

Yannick heard the swish of Anja's skiing parka. I hope she kept the delivery pouch, too, he thought, thinking of the congealed cheesy soufflé she would find inside it.

They people filed out in two lines, calling out goodbyes to each other, down two different tunnels, and then the cavern was empty.

After thirty or forty minutes of steady pacing, Yannick and Anja's line stopped. They stood still, like the obedient prisoners they were. Since her ordeal with the fatberg, Anja hadn't spoken. In the bunker no one had wanted to approach the girl. She had been given water to wash her hands and face, but it hadn't begun to remove the fetor.

If she was repellant, he was standoffish. He didn't know what to say to her and stood back, sparing his own nostrils.

"Where will you go from here, Homeless?"

It was the voice of the man behind him, who had orchestrated the dark theatre of the last four days appropriating one of the world's capital cities as his stage, but it might have been Yannick's own subconscious talking.

"Are we getting out?"

"We are."

"No idea," said Yannick. His spell in the underworld had been an interlude between nothing and nothing.

"You can stay at mine. I have a sofa-bed. I'll even give you work. You can be my dog!" said Sven.

The line started shifting forwards. One by one, people were climbing or being helped up a ladder.

"Great," said Yannick, with all the irony of his irrelevant self, knowing it was the best and only offer he had. "Alright."

When it was her turn, Anya reached up and found the ladder, which consisted of lengths of rebar bent round and cemented into the wall. She declined any help from below and pulled herself up hand over hand, until she got her feet on the bottom rung and could push up.

It was close to ten in the morning when they emerged from a lottery kiosk in the financial district and found themselves on a snowing street, deserted but for a vanishing line of blind people, the anonymous last of whom carried a cat box. All the lights remained out and it was still night, but Yannick and Anja suddenly sensed light with all the pressure of a solid. It was as if the door of the kiosk had opened to an irrepressible tsunami of information in bits and bytes, which they still could not compute. Like purblind, newborn mice, pallid and uncertain, they peered round at the pavement and the buildings and breathed in the freezing fresh air.

"Hurry along, can't stop," ordered Sven.

Anja and Yannick aimed bleary eyes at each other, squinting like mad people.

He had grime smeared over an unshaven face and still wore his multicoloured jacket like some unfortunate harlequin.

Her reintroduction to the world-above-ground was a cruel one. Not only was she soiled and shocked from her encounter with the fatberg, but she was also shivering violently. A stiff breeze blowing up the street had her at its mercy. The once beige felt coat, slimy with the fatberg's putrid gunk, was a wet weight over her thin tops. It was all she had left.

Yannick took off his polychrome padded coat to wrap her in it. She stepped back, refusing it and him. She could not be touched.

"Shall I come with you?" he said.

"No," she shook her head. She wasn't sure how, but one way or another she would make it to her mother's. On her own. Away from all of it.

"Are you going to be alright?"

"Go," she said.

Yannick went, after the tramping Sven who was already disappearing into the murk, after a promise of work and a refuge. When he looked back and Anja was no longer there, a sense of panic seized him and he cursed himself for letting the girl go off on her own in the state that she and the city were in. The extravagant coat that protected him from the elements felt a badge of dishonour. He threw the cap that Sven had given him across the street, as if petulant sacrifice might achieve anything at all. There was a lot of garbage on the street and he heard something that he had previously only heard in movies: distant gunfire.

Yannick's brain was busily configuring the new visual set-up. The contrast with the utter absence of light in the blind underground was enough for him to make out shapes and surfaces as if there were early daylight. Either that, or Sven swinging his new wand was casting light all about. Yannick caught up with him and they went quickly up the street together and through the financial district, where their way was hampered here and there by snow drifts banked up against abandoned SDVs. All had all been broken into and more than one of them wrecked and burned. Yannick marvelled at the texture of the snow, the sight of his own hands, the purple-black icicles hanging from road signs, and the unrivalled spatial advantage of experiencing reality in visual 3D thanks to just a handful of photons.

Sven allowed himself to be steered in order to gather pace through the snow, but it was bringing them closer to a fracas with ugly shouting and a crackling that was happening just around the next corner on the right. It was projecting a lively, flickering glow.

"Straight on, don't stop," gasped Sven, who no longer seemed as fit and confident as he had been in the underworld. He stamped forwards with his stick and briefcase like Mr Magoo. They reached the street corner and Yannick held back, mesmerized by the oranges and yellows of a building on fire. A group of men stood there defiantly, staring at their work and urging each other on.

"Oi! What you got there?" called one of them and set off on a run at Sven, some twenty metres away and brightly lit by the fulminating blaze.

An easy target.

"Oh gods!" thought Yannick. He might have few favourable feelings towards Sven, but after everything the leader of the blind had achieved, it seemed plain wrong that he should be robbed of his main prize and most likely hurt in the process. Besides, the man was his only hope.

He moved fast to put himself between Sven and his attacker, who stopped, facing him.

"You're fucked," the man said, coming at him.

Yannick, who was lankier but taller, launched himself forwards and stuck two outstretched fingers into his opponent's eyes. The man screamed and staggered backwards. Yannick grabbed Sven's arm and propelled him onwards and away. The other men, instead of coming to their comrade's aid, joked and laughed at his expense, and soon the darkness swallowed the two escapees up once more.

"Where are we going?" said Yannick, rather less deferential now, pulling the older man along.

"Five blocks east and ten north," said Sven. "Let go of me."

Yannick's heart drummed wildly. To the elation of bettering their attacker and getting away was now joined a known and reachable destination. They were going to make it.

. . . .

In the sewer-tunnel complex beneath their feet, the search team had quickly discovered the plotters' artifice and pushed through the gap in the wall that Yannick had blocked inexpertly and in haste. Knowing which way to go from there was another matter. However, to their good fortune, Anja's thread, immediately apparent to their strong flashlights, proved a reliable guide all the way to what been the HQ of the operation, but which was now empty save for an odd arrangement of ropes and seating, a few items of clothing, small bags of trash and a table with unwashed plates, water bottles, bread, cheese and a half-finished mug of black coffee. The coffee was still lukewarm. Three other tunnels led off from the capacious underground den and agents were sent running to explore them all while the team leader radioed in.

"They've always almost got him," commented the mayor.

"Not just him. There's evidence of a concentration of people down there," said Zoltan.

"Do we really not have a positive ID for our man?" said the PM.

Zoltan shook his head. "We ran a DNA check on a hair we cut from him and he's not on any databank. But we'll track him down."

"Prime Minister, was that signed document for real? I mean: is it legally obliging and valid?" asked the mayor.

"Of course," she said. "In the end, he didn't ask for that much and I don't think that the destruction of our country was worth taking a gamble on, do you?"

The mayor's eyes went from the mounting box of of crisis reports on his desk to the rising number of fatalities marked on a whiteboard.

"Team One, Team One," crackled the radio. " We have something. It was left under the coffee mug."

A harshly illuminated image of a hand-drawn sketch appeared on a monitor screen in the mayoral office. It depicted a network with a nucleus clearly marked just off-centre and five large red crosses.

"Those are the cut-off points. Call back the search parties," Zoltan instructed the force leader, "and send in the engineers. Give them copies of that map and an escort and let me know immediately you find anything. The human objectives can wait."

• • • •

In an eastern district of the city, weary, bunkered-down people were preparing what meagre meal they still had, or lay around wrapped in all their clothes and blankets to withstand the brutal freeze inside their homes, when a little after midday, sirens began to wail, lightbulbs exploded and domestic appliances came to life as the electrical supply was restored. It crashed immediately with the shock of the overload, but an hour later, the engineers had it up and running again. By six pm, the other sectors of the city were back on electrical power also. The Prime Minister broadcast a message to celebrate the brave and accomplished work of engineers in repairing the unprecedented power failure, to promise a thorough, in-depth investigation, and send the most special Christmas greetings to all the country's citizens, their families and friends.

No mention was made of sabotage and certainly nothing of a blind ringleader and his underground organization.

In a follow-up message, she enumerated a broad package of emergency measures as well as longer-term plans to get the capital back on its feet again, with particular help for the disadvantaged, such as the old, the housebound and the blind.

Sven heard the broadcast in his first floor apartment, where Yannick was deeply asleep in an armchair. Ha! They're going public with it, Sven realized, so that I don't. That way they save face.

He gave his human guide dog a nudge with his boot. "Pisshead," he said loudly. He could hardly call him Homeless now. "We did it!"

Yannick didn't stir. He was lost to a realm of dreams in which his feet were made of lead blocks and he could not speak. He stood rooted to the spot in the central concourse of a mall, waving helplessly to passing shoppers who thought he was part of the mall entertainment. High above his head, coloured lights twinkled in the ceiling, calling to him but unable to fall. He would have to climb the central palm and shake them loose. Yannick slept on.

Elsewhere in the reconnected city, the relief was widespread but the jubilation muted. People saw and stared at each other, church bells rang and everyone waited doggedly for electronic devices to charge, central heating radiators to get warm and water cisterns to heat up. The planned Christmas Eve celebrations had long been forsaken, but it didn't really matter when you were going to live.

Sven warned Yannick to expect a knock on the door, but when none came that night or the next morning, Yannick felt inexplicably guilty. He put their clothes through a wash-and-dry cycle, so that both men would at least be clean and presentable for their arrest. He himself looked almost respectable in his new haircut. Another day passed and another and still nothing happened and nobody came for them.

• • • •

It was a place to stay. Yannick's duties were light, simple housecleaning, some of the cooking, putting away shopping and bringing Sven coffee in his recliner after a mid-morning nap. That and keeping an eye out for unusual activity outside.

The newsfeed continued to report on pockets of the city where power was still out and people had been moved to emergency accommodation with medical attention and a debacle in the bid to restock warehouses and food stores. Orders for Sven's larder and fridge-freezer, however, turned up in minutes at a shake of his magic stick. The administration was clearly making sure, until they felt confident that the situation was stable, that the blind would be pampered.

Sven paid Yannick generously from his newly restored state benefit, but a despondency came over him that only deepened.

The demon of depression wanted to suck him down its vortex and hold him prisoner indefinitely. To Sven's lively talk, he responded monosyllabically or in grunts. He was, he acknowledged, reverting to his old, familiar self. The one who saw no way out.

At the end of a week in which the only excursion, after Sven discovered his factotum's professional studies, had been to a library, where the blind man took out four crime novels and a romance, Yannick waved his arms around and declared that he could not bear to be cooped up any longer. Sven gave him the day off and told him to not to worry about shopping or cooking. The meals service SDVs were back in action, so dinner was taken care of. He told his home help to empty the dishwasher and beat it.

On a whim, missing his bike keenly, Yannick decided to go back to where he had last seen and left it, propped against an iron bench opposite the lottery kiosk. He donned his coat which was still reassuringly snug, if battered and torn in places and the colours faded by a hot wash, closed the door quietly and bounded down the stairs to the foyer and out to the street. He was glad that it was a long walk from Sven's and so put a distance between them.

He came to the old square and walked straight in. It was more obviously lit than ever before, but no longer cordoned off. Looking over, he saw that the barricades that Anja had told him about remained in place around the entrances and exits of public buildings; yet the greater part of the precinct was transited once again by cautious, subdued citizens.

The kiosk was still there and the bench, if not his bicycle. He went over and sat down where he had before, scanning the environs on the off-chance that his bike might still be around, or the bottle of schnapps even, a dropped glove: any evidence, anything at all, that it had all really happened. The kiosk wasn't giving anything away. He observed the closed booth with a sense that it owed him something. The implausibility of his incarceration unnerved him. Even if his mind knew that it had been real, he couldn't eradicate from it the wild suggestion that the missing bicycle invalidated that theory. Maybe the woman at the Social Security was right. Maybe he did have a mental health issue, a major one. How would he know? Perhaps something more credible but far worse had happened to him, a psychotic event followed by memory loss and he had invented the narrative to protect himself from the truth. It was not, he knew, a reasonable hypothesis. The bicycle would have been stolen anyway, even if the city hadn't deteriorated to a riotous hell and policing the streets become an impossibility. What was reasonable, then? And what good would it do him?

He dug his cold hands into the coat's deep pockets. There was a small, lumpy object at the bottom of one of them. He drew it out and stared, overcome by a giddy bout of remembering, at the domino. Double three. The girl must have slipped it into his pocket. The undulating beautician. It meant, he remembered to recall, whatever you found it to mean. A double had a power, he decided, and two threes equalled throwing a six, meaning you had another go.

He went over to the nearest police unit, the one superintending the public entrance to the Town Hall, and walked up to the guard.

"It's about a bicycle," he said.

He explained how he had left it in the square the day of the blackout.

"Unlocked, you say. When all the lights went out, over a week ago," the officer said, while two others looked him up and down. The interruption was even more tiresome than the guard duty itself. The armed officer sighed and told him to stay where he was. He spoke briefly on an intercom and came back with a look of some surprise on his face.

"Well, it seems there is one," he said. "What colour is it?"

"Black and white," Yannick said. "On the back of the saddle there's a sticker of a Vulkan greeting."

He raised a hand to show what he meant.

"Lower your hand," warned the officer, but afterwards went back to the intercom.

It turned out that throughout the widespread disturbances of the blackout, the sealed-off square had been the safest and most secure place of all. It had been cleared of the public, squatting vagrants and all unjustifiable objects or personal property, some of which remained confiscated. The police had three mobile devices, two umbrellas, one pair of reading glasses, one shopping trolley, one car key, a bag of Christmas shopping, a handbag and a bicycle.

Minutes later, Yannick felt like he had been handed back his only true friend in the world. He rode off in some glee, cycling this way and that with no plan in mind, moving through the gears, going nowhere in the city's own pointless warren, welcoming the sense of speed and even the freezing air that made his eyes stream.

When he got back to Sven's, he carried his bicycle up the stairs and wheeled it clickety-click into the apartment hallway to rest it against the wall. His host was busily voice-programming his new stick, but broke off to tell him:

"I'm kicking you out. Nothing personal, you understand, but I'm getting one of these bots. You see, I don't like to feel that anyone is here on sufferance. And you are. The bot will do more than I can ever ask of you at any time of day or night and they have very nice voices. Or you can mute the voice. They don't lie in a huddled lump on the sofa. Anyway, give me the key when you go. The dosh on the entrance table is what I owe you."

"So that's it? You mean now?"

"Listen. There are less than two thousand people in this city registered as blind. It's only a matter of time before they track me down and when they do, they'll get you as an accessory. No matter what your protestations of being a hapless hostage, here you are cohabiting with the ringleader. And we were on the same course together, remember? An electronics course. So on yer bike. Get lost. Clear off while you still can."

"What will happen to you?"

"Me? They'll slap me about a bit, I imagine. Ask me the same dumb questions a hundred times and eventually come to realize that we, the sightless, bested the seers. No terrorists, no unhinged fanatics, no foreign interference, just a bunch of blind cunts. They can send me to prison: I don't care. But they'll probably drop it. The humiliation in the press would be too much. The government order agreeing our demands is a legal document that cannot be denied and that's what they'll be after, but they won't find it when they search here. When we went to the library, I stashed it in the Braille section, where I reckon it's safe. Even so, after a while, they'll start to go back on their concessions, like the sneaky, cowardly fuckers they are, until we have little left but a stick." Sven waved his around.

"So why do it?" Yannick was already in the hallway, where he righted his bicycle by its handlebar.

"You know why."

Yannick looked over to the dead-eyed pensioner, hunched forward in an armchair that seemed too small for him, holding the cyberstick across his knees.

" We wanted you to see us. To feel we exist. We wanted our day in the black sun. Goodbye, Yannick."

· · · ·

Outside, storm cloud was massing over a drab late morning, but Yannick had no mind to hurry. He paused to listen and look around. The unrest and disturbances had given way to a manageable unease and in this well-to-do neighbourhood, at least, it was quiet. The street lights were on and there was nobody running or shouting. The semblance of normality had returned. Electrical power had been back on for almost a week and the seductive powers of internet and central heating were keeping most people indoors, lying low, with New Year's Eve on the morrow.

A blackbird sitting on a bare aspen branch ruffled its feathers assertively and blinked. It was meanly cold and Yannick wished he hadn't lost his gloves and thrown away the cap. He got on his bicycle and pushed off on what seemed one and the same, if interrupted, ride from the last place he wasn't wanted to nowhere in particular. He still hadn't been sacked. Discontinued, released, disconnected and now kicked out.

He felt liberated, if not free. At least he had some krona to see him through the next couple of weeks. He cycled through the slate grey air to the end of the road and waited for a family to cross, before turning left up the avenue.

There was some light traffic. A few delivery vehicles had come back to electronic life, intent on reclaiming the roads with their predictable, optimistic milling around, yet hampered by having to manoeuvre cumbersomely around frozen vans and taxis, like ants around dead companions. Yannick stretched his legs and weaved past them.

There were other signs that things were still not right.

He could see strangers in a rebooted passenger vehicle talking animatedly to each other. People just didn't do that. And a young girl with bright red hair, on her way to visit cousins with late Christmas presents, was having to wait on the sidewalk while her mother and father embraced someone they had chanced upon in the street in a way they never had done before, hugging them tight and long. It was Nordic introversion turned inside out.

There were quite a few people out, pressing forwards against the remorseless cold, willing themselves with each pace to forget and move on, discovering that stores were reopening and it was safe to queue outside them, but there was still no bread to be had, no butter or milk, let alone turkey or pork for a New Year's roast. Some pasta, maybe. A few scrawny vegetables. A can of soup. They were shopping for hope, with the cold stone of recent memory in their bellies.

It was still the Christmas holidays and Yannick could hear these people wanting to believe. Explaining away the last few days as a unique event (which it surely was), a fault that had been put right. Normal service was being resumed. They would all pick up from where they left off and carry on.

But it wasn't the same city. These seemly, unexcitable people who thrived and depended on uneventful, everyday continuity knew that it could no longer be counted on. Security and assured well-being were supposed to be inviolable and now that social pledge had been compromised, the illusion shown up all too blatantly. To Yannick, it was as if his subjective experience of the world had somehow emerged to be shared by everyone else, which was hardly his wish. He could understand what these people were going through, but he couldn't feel at home in it, either. He stopped for a minute outside a pet shop, blowing on his hands and rubbing them. There were no live animals on display in the window. They had rights these days. Did Abegael get her farmdog, he wondered? Did Silky the cat make it out safely? They would probably never know. He wrote and sent a short message to Anja on his mobile and received a thumbs up.

He had to take a wide berth of a corner coffee shop where a small crowd was spilling back anxiously into the avenue. A fight had broken out among the clients waiting to get in and now the manager was out, closing up hurriedly, boarding up the windows again. Yannick cycled on, driving the pedals to speed up: not to go and collect his things from the bedsit, or even to sleep on a warm floor, although he would gladly accept it, but to talk, if she would do that, with the only person who might hear him.

• • • •

Anja's apartment was, if such a thing were possible (and she would always find something to clean or rearrange) more immaculate than ever. Four days had gone by since she had accompanied her mother and Granma Osa in a taxi to the bus station and during that time she had only left home only once, to buy what basic foodstuffs and cheap clothing she could from the empty stores. Otherwise, she had been alone, washing, wiping, scouring, dusting, tidying, to a music playlist that no longer charmed her, or simply standing with her back to a hot radiator, waiting for her mind to unfreeze and coalesce to its former, healthy keenness and composure.

On finding herself alone and freezing fast on the street when Yannick and all the blind had gone, she had veered off from her original course to her mother's and made for home. Even if by going straight there she could save them from death's door, her family could not see her like this. Over and above which, her apartment was considerably closer and she was in a parlous state. When she finally arrived at the steps leading up to it, she wanted, against all reasonable expectation, but willing it all the same, the security light to come on. It didn't. But when she climbed the steps and turned the mechanical key in the lock, the building let her in.

The apartment was numbingly cold, but she had had no choice. In the bathroom, in pitch darkness that she no longer found a hindrance, she painstakingly removed her fouled clothing and double-bagged it for disposal. The shower that should have rained hot, blessed relief tortured her shaking body instead with an excruciating stream that Anja could only endure by means of crying and curses that she sincerely hoped the neighbours could hear. Afterwards, her hair had been rid of a stickiness the consistency of vomit and her skin soaped and rinsed twice. She was still in tears when she put on layers of clean clothing, her warmest items all now lost, and sat on the bed, her very own bed, rocking compulsively, while her hair dried under a thick towel. She could still smell the stench.

She went out wrapped in a blanket and walked two kilometres to her mother's, where found Osa and Mamma alive but motionless in the stone-cold dark of the charred living room. They were sitting on a mattress and propped against the wall by cushions, under a heap of clothing and duvets that were pulled up to their pale chins.

They had looked up at her arrival in a mixture of happiness and dull disbelief and could not speak. She automatically went to make them a hot tea until she realized the obviousness that there was no electric. She wondered when was the last time that the women ate. More worryingly, no water came out of the taps. The unwashed plates and dishes in the kitchen hadn't been used for some time. All the canned foods, soup, goulash, red cabbage, herring, green beans had gone. They had chewed the raw potatoes, too. There was only uncooked rice and pasta left, along with undrinkable coffee and tea.

All that she could think to do was comfort them. I'm-here-now. It's-all-going-to-be-alright. Certain that she still reeked of the fatberg was knowledge that pushed her close to a flighty madness and she even laughed. Osa waved a bony finger at her linen bag on the floor. Anja found that her grandmother's purse contained banknotes, quite a lot of them. She grabbed her mother's warmest coat and went out. Half an hour later, she was back with water and some dry biscuits, which the three women shared in silence. Afterwards, Anja had emptied the crumbs in her hand into the fireplace and rejoined the older women under the quilts.

When, hours later, the electricity came on with a jolt for less than five seconds and then went off again and didn't come back, Anja could almost have cared less. Perhaps it was better that they should not be seen, not see each like this. Only when it came on and stayed on, filling the kitchen with shocking white light, and illuminating the red spot that said that the water cistern was heating, did she let go and cry. Meanwhile, the boiler in the basement was whooshing into action, beginning to circulate cold water to the building's radiators that would soon be lukewarm and then hot.

The older women, strengthened by mutual resolve, sipping hot, sweet, black tea, told Anja that they would leave for Osa's cottage in the country as soon as it was humanly possible. Of course, thought Anja, knowing the small bounty that Osa's garden could produce, its faithful well and stock of firewood. Who wouldn't want to leave this city? It took her mother and a shaky Grandma Osa two full days, until the twenty-sixth, to be steady enough to make the journey, which was also the first day that seats on a bus could be secured. Anastasia hadn't looked back at her wrecked home, its furniture burned as if by squatters, its promise of permanence dashed. Anja waved them off at the bus station, now operating a strictly limited service under a watchful army presence, two refugees fleeing to safety from a terrible regime. She herself had taken another taxi home.

Since when she had had little else to occupy her other than compulsive showering and housecleaning, since her mobile, once plugged in and updated, informed her she that no longer had a job, a boyfriend, or the basement studio.

Julian had broken off with her by texting *I feel we should just leave it there. Pls rtn pass* after she had failed to answer two messages of his and a call. The curt dismissal of their brief relationship made her all the more aggrieved for the relief it gave her. Lacking either the romance of an encounter or the jollity that went with a fling, it had felt like cultivating a convenient arrangement. She knew it, knew that she should have known better. But she deserved better than this.

Her company had emblazoned its severance notice with the announcement that innovation and investment in data would mark a major advance in the New Year. A development that she was clearly expected to approve and even be proud of. A phone call to a colleague confirmed Anja's suspicion. She'd been AI'd. The insurance company was replacing human resources with apps and bots. Businesses would now enter the relevant data on an app, which would calculate the policy price and offer to set up a direct debit. If the business had its own bot for cleaning and security purposes, as more and more did, then its cameras and scanners could be appropriated by the insurance company once a year to check compliance with health and safety regulations, borrowing the bot and directing it around the working environment.

As for the studio apartment, when she had missed the mortgage payment, the bank had swiftly and greedily repossessed it.

Only a week ago, she would have risen up against such adversity. She would have moved heaven and earth to turn back the tide and come out of it on top, like the supersurfing winner she was. For that Anja, to be out of control of her finances was unforgiveable. It meant she was out of control of her life. There was simply no excuse. But that Anja didn't need to keep the lights on all night or else she couldn't sleep. She hadn't been ingested or defiled by something unspeakable. That Anja didn't know that heaven was empty of gods, that there were none to save you once the hungry earth had gobbled you up, none to hear your singing. You could only hope to hell that it might spit you out again.

Not all was black night, but somehow it kept seeping back in.

Even though Granma Osa had insisted on putting a wad of money into her hand, a Christmas extra to "tide her over," her bank balance remained precariously low. She could get by for a while, two, maybe three months, she calculated. It would be double that, but her winning ticket, the lottery card with its ample payout, was lodged somewhere in a buttoned pocket of her coat and there it would stay, legible or not, bagged up in the garbage container next to the boiler room, until the refuse collectors came to take the vile ruin away for incineration.

What she really needed was a new job. When she networked out to contacts and friends, such as she had, for another position, the effort yielded apologetic nothings, but more alarming to her was the half-heartedness that was the most she could put into the search. She was too restless. She couldn't focus. She was too nervous to go out. When she dug her heels in mentally, there was no terra firma and she desisted before they sank into something like quicksand. She could only eat and watch TV, and wanted to, so she stayed in and did that.

• • • •

The Tuesday after Mamma and Osa left, Anja decided to resurrect her old life, starting with a fondue evening. The boiler was functioning unerringly and even she had to admit that by now, an entire litre of gel and shampoo and two sponges later, she was probably clean and presentable.

She invited round a couple she was friendly with from the singing group, who met her at the door with big smiles that in the space of two hours turned into expressions of concern and darting looks at each other, before they made their excuses, said thanks for a lovely meal, patted her on the back, congratulated her on the Japanese bonsai and got away. They had never seen their health-conscious friend drink before, let alone two large gins, and they had certainly not heard her so blunt and challenging, asking what they really felt "underneath it all." What it was they really wanted.

One of the men attempted to calm things down. "Anja, you've been through a lot, everyone has," he said. "It takes time to get over the shock, I think. One of our neighbours got stuck in a lift for the blackout and died there, from the cold or hunger, I don't know which." "Oh, that's terrible," said Anja. "Did you eat him? I mean: did you find him?" There was a brief silence. "The firemen found him," said the other man. He cleared his throat. "What about you, Anja? How did you spend the blackout?"

The next morning, a hungover Anja had had to clean the apartment again, and then go for such a run through the long streets that her lungs were burning and she threw up behind a bush.

She hadn't done any more socializing after that.

She knew that she wasn't alright and wondered briefly if she should seek counselling, until she realized that she would only find herself relating the same events to the same wide-eyed or wary sympathy, when what she really needed was corroboration. Someone else who heard the heavy city breathing in the shadows, mouthing its fear and its secrets. Someone she could show the black ink sketches that she had made with a name under one. The Wolf. The Witch. The Beast. Almost Normal. The Bat.

Today, she was more collected. She had spoken to Mamma and Osa on the phone and they were doing just fine, baking potatoes in the fireplace at the farmhouse. A duck was hanging in the barn, out of reach of foxes, in readiness for the year's farewell dinner.

Her own home was now acceptably tidy. The only items that bothered her, for being extraneous and unresolved, were her tenant's belongings and a glossy folder that lay on the sideboard, next to a postcard. Now that she had just received a message from him and he was coming round, most of it would presumably soon be gone.

The postcard was from Yannick's father. He wouldn't be coming back. He and Miguel were making a new life together. The fresh fish was wonderful. The photo showed palm trees and a turquoise ocean and, like a prop from another movie altogether, it didn't belong in her apartment.

It was about time he came round for his things, she decided. It had been a week since they parted after their joyless escape. The old year had only one more day in it. Anja felt unappreciated, even if she had evicted him and only invited him back in her own mind to a bedsit that was no longer hers to offer.

Her eyes went to the folder. It was her present from Julian, the pass for the coming year to elite spa and sauna hotels in locations of outstanding natural beauty. Once she had figured out what *Pls rtn pass* meant, she realized that she was being told to action a memo. Very well, it would be the elegant thing to do. One of them reimbursed and the other unbeholden. A clean break, she told herself, going to her office stationery for an envelope.

Which is when a stream of invective in her father's dialect, but her own voice, rushed out of her with a directness of expression and a choice vocabulary. It was all over in a matter of seconds, enough, nonetheless, for her to know that an unscheduled arraignment had just taken place and that Julian's case was disesteemed.

She slipped the envelope back into its cellophane pack. Was this the new Anja, she wondered? Where would it all lead?

Following which, she had opened and read through the folder's contents three times. There were upgrade options to silver, gold and platinum, which cost a small fortune, but this bronze pass gave you four free nights per month at any hotel or hotels, breakfast and dinner, plus the spa baths, sauna with massage (once each) and aromatherapy. A pair of platinum-coloured wristbands that gave you all the frills for the first visit were held by nylon ties to stiff, shiny cardboard with a sunny, colour photograph, an aerial view of a remote cliff complex with gardens overlooking a turquoise green fjord.

The year's pass for two people, the gift that Julian wanted returned so that he could use it on someone else, was a bronze plastic card printed with the logo of the spa-hotel chain and her name in raised letters. The letter in the pack confirmed that the pass was for her plus one, without naming Julian, who would reasonably enough have assumed that he was the one and no one but him. It could be anyone, though.

She had already toyed with the idea of taking Granma Osa, who would be round the kitchen asking where they kept their chickens and picking off dead heads in the rose garden, while she herself read a book in a white lounge with more plate glass window than wall, raising her eyes to gaze across a lawn that ended in a cliff-edge gazebo, wondering why she, at twenty-five, not unattractive, hadn't found anyone to go with her. She would willingly send them both together, Mamma and Granma, to soak in the spa pools and be served smoked trout, but no, it had to be the person whose name was on the card: Anja. Anja plus one.

It was, she thought, a chance.

The luxury leisure industry remained hands-on, rather than tech-driven, with people paying to be attended by other, real people, not bots and devices. She could retrain as a masseuse, or as a fitness instructor in the resort gyms. If she started now, she could learn and qualify to teach yoga in as little as three months. Or aerobics, say, or biodance, or breathing techniques. Maybe they would even let her sing in the hotel lounge... There were thirteen spa locations, which gave her thirteen opportunities for connecting with managements and finding out what was in demand, giving a presentation of her services and making an impression.

The forest took your darkness and gave yourself back, Yannick had told her. Several of the locations offered opportunities for guided bike rides through the natural wilds of the surroundings. So they had a need for specialist bicycle guides. It could be just the thing for him. If he wanted, of course. It wasn't as if they had anything. What was it that he wanted to see her about?

Anja stood at the window. He had been at least ten minutes already. She could tidy the magazines from the sofa, but he wouldn't care, wouldn't even notice, or pick one up and find something interesting in it.

There he was.

"Ha!" Anja said to the apartment. He had sunk away but she had drawn him back on her string, raised his submarine from the ocean's sucking jaw.

She watched him padlock his bicycle to the railing, take a look at what had been his apartment and walk up the steps to press the buzzer. He pulled off his bicycle helmet and tucked it under his arm like a fencer's visor. His long hair was stylishly cropped. Had he changed? She let him in and went to open her apartment door.

His footsteps echoed as he mounted the stairs and stopped when he saw her standing in the doorway above him. A sudden noise from the second floor—something heavy, dropped and rolling on a wooden floor—distracted their attention briefly before they made eye contact again.

Go on, she waited. Say the words I want to hear.

Yannick opened his mouth and took a breath.

"I lost my job again," he said.

Did you love *Citizens of the Night*? Then you should read *The Ministry of Flowers*[1] by Guy Arthur Simpson!

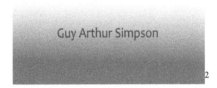

Lorenzo is worried about the city.

Everyone else is worried about Lorenzo.

Decay and chaos blight the sprawling metropolis and he suspects that the flowers are to blame. Although maybe the cardboard collectors are mixed up in it as well.

The President will know—and Lorenzo means to find out.

novella ~ 76 pages

Read more at www.guysimpson.com.

---

1. https://books2read.com/u/bpOzjJ

2. https://books2read.com/u/bpOzjJ